The Deposition

By

Katherine E. Kreuter

RISING TIDE PRESS

Rising Tide Press
3831 N. Oracle Road
Tucson, AZ 85705
520-888-1140

Printed in the United States on acid-free paper.

Publisher's note:
All characters, places, and situations in this book are
fictitious, or used fictitiously, and any resemblance
to persons (living or dead) is purely coincidental.

Cover art by Jude Ockenfels

First Printing: July 2000

        Kreuter, Katherine E.
        The Deposition/Katherine E. Kreuter

ISBN 1-883061-30-X

Library of Congress Control Number: 00 133935

DEDICATION
For
Monique

ACKNOWLEDGEMENTS

The author wishes to thank Karen Mayers, Scott Page Anderson, Kim Miltenberger, Marilyn Ravicz, Ann Miller, Lee Boojamra, and Alice Frier for their critiques and encouragement.

The Deposition

By

Katherine E. Kreuter

PROLOGUE

"Aim high!" Dad always told me. At the time I thought I knew what he meant, but as I write this today I'm not so sure. I'm not sure of anything anymore, thanks to Simone. My dear Simone Franklin: the *raison d'être* of my novel, the love of my life.

Simone will tell you that I always went too far. And I still wonder if it wasn't Dad's "Aim High!" that planted that wild seed in me. Little Salmon is what he used to call me. He said I was the fish that broke water, flip-flopped up into the air and fought my way upstream, to where the action was. No matter what.

It all started one silly summer morning when I was about three feet tall and looking for action in the alley behind our house. Dickie Halloway burst out of the bushes, stuck his BB gun in my face and yelled, "Bang!" I slugged him for upstaging me like that, but in minutes we were pals again, and that was the day I named us Gang Bang. It was also the day we went off on our first lark. While Mrs. McPhail was out in her garage for a few minutes, we slipped into her house and streaked off with a pair of her Tahitian panties and bra. Then the next evening, while the Ridgeways were out, we squeezed in through one of their basement windows and stashed our treasures in Mr. Ridgeway's laundry bag. You should have heard Mrs. Ridgeway on Monday morning! Dickie and I did, even from under an elm tree a block away.

Simone thought that was a weird thing to do, probably because she never had any real childhood herself. But I know she loved my little grabber, because the day she heard it she nicknamed me G.B., short for Gang Banger.

All my life, I wanted wild. You can have your garden-variety thrills like hang gliding or race cars or (Hugh Grant's) Divine pick-ups in Hollywood. The business world with its computer- controlled bucks and brains never seduced me either. Too tame. Too cut and dried. My schemes were academic, if you will. Meaning was my thing, not money. I'd take lark over loot every time.

I finally reached a point where I couldn't any longer dream up a scheme crazy enough to match my cravings. Not until I met Simone, that is. That's when I began to concoct the caper of capers.

Long before I took her to Paris, I was preparing her for The Big One -- whetting her appetite for raw adventure. At first some of my schemes scandalized her. She even told me that my father's business had no doubt had a major effect on my formative years. In fact, she nearly left me when she heard about it. Dad turned horses into dogs, you see, and there was no David Copperfield magic to it. I watched it all as a child. First they blinded the horse in one eye so it couldn't see the man with the rifle. Then they sent it down a runway and shot it. The choice parts were canned for human consumption and shipped to France; the rest became dog food. Zip, zap, zup.

And bye bye, Black Beauty.

This is a subject that I always tried to avoid with Simone, horsewoman and animal lover that she is. "How could you, G.B.?" she'd squeal. How could I what? "Be part of it?" What did she think? I pulled the trigger? Simone could spout all that holierthanthou litany to me, standing in the checkout line at the supermarket with a shopping cart full of Ken-L-Ration for her own canines. And with *her* family history!

But don't get me wrong; I love horses, too. And so do the French, who also know the value of their precious flesh.Far more tender and tasty than beef, it's obviously more costly because there's not as much edible meat on a horse.Given that, an idiot can figure out that if a horse is slaughtered for human consumption, there's a lot of waste.

Back in the roaring twenties, my father -- who, by the way, was born in the brutal Minnesotan winter of 1880 and had reached the ripe age of sixty-five the year his young secretary-cum-wife gave birth to me -- gave a lot of thought to that waste. He turned the leftovers into what was probably the first pet food ever produced.

Dad should have made millions, sitting on top of that fledgling gold mine. He should have moved us on to yachts and private jets and Picassos and numbered Viennese bank accounts. But he and Mom ended up where they started: in our three-bedroom house in a nice heartland neighborhood with sidewalks and elm trees. If you define boredom as the repetition of the same perceptual field, then Boredom is where I grew up. State and Main and church on Sundays.

You can have it.

Eventually, Dad blew the family fortune on junk bonds and then blew his brains out. My mother wasn't long in following him to Elsewhere. That left me flip-flopping on my own: a Big Salmon at last, leaping her way upstream, anxious for action.

Simone would tell you that I should have learned to walk on water instead.

But I wonder now if maybe I've been going through life more like Dad's horses running the plank, blinded in one eye. Seeing only the lighter half of reality. Ignoring my fate, which was perhaps obvious to any innocent observer.

Maybe.

You be the judge.

CHAPTER ONE

"The biggest bed in all Paris!"

The year is 1985. It's April in Paris. I am sitting on a bench in one of the downstairs rooms of the Marmottan Museum, in meditation mode, waiting for the right moment to pop my plan.

Across the room, Simone is standing in her painterly pose in front of Claude Monet's *Impression Sunrise*, the painting that gave Impressionism its name. An imaginary brush in hand, she is squinting on and off at it as if she needed glasses. But those eyes are 20/20. Big brown Irish eyes that catapulted me across a crowded room the first time ever I saw her face, if you'll pardon the sweaty lyrics.

Svelte as a scimitar and smashing in an old-gold dress, Simone is now rocking back and forth on one high heel and tossing her head in quirky little jerks. In Boredom that would get her more than covert glances and fingers tapped to foreheads. But in a place like Paris and the Marmottan, nobody pays any attention. Except for the one guard in the room. Monsieur is mesmerized by Simone's chestnut hair that reaches down to the middle of her back and is now swishing about like a horse's tail. I could probably walk off with my bench and he wouldn't notice. But then I'm obviously not his type: too tall and too lean, hair too short and too dark, pantsuit too somber and too tailored.

Too bad.

I wonder what Monsieur would say if I told him where Simone's hypnotizing hair had been early morning....

He finally shuffles into the adjacent room -- awash in Monet's water lilies -- and Simone finally drifts over to my bench.

"This place is dynamite," she gushes.

This place, which Simone is seeing today for the first time, is located at No. 2, rue Louis-Boilly, a stone's throw from the Bois de Boulogne, in the tony 16th arrondissement. In 1932, the art historian Paul Marmottan left the house and original collection of Renaissance sculpture and tapestry and Empire things to the State. Claude Monet's son, Michel, subsequently gave the museum some sixty-five paintings by his father.

From the moment you step inside here it's "optical arrest," as Simone put it. Downstairs with the Monets, that is. Upstairs, you can forget the Empire painting and furniture, "much of it godawful, that pinched little 18th century art," according to Simone. "Empire crap."

She sits down, smack up against me now, and emits a low, orgasmic moan that again recalls our early morning. I seize the moment.

"Want to take *Impression Sunrise* home with us?" rolls off my tongue like mercury down a pane of glass.

"Sure!" she giggles. "Let's take the Mon-ey and run!"

I ignore her Grade B pun. "We could hang a Simone Franklin original in its place. A forgery. You could do it, right?"

"A copy? Old stuff. Art school. Forget it." She shakes her head. "When you go to the slammer, G.B., you're going alone."

"But there's not going to be any crime."

"Say again?"

"Look, if I were to put Ken-L-Ration in your steak and kidney pie and you couldn't taste the difference, would there be any crime?" That line was unrehearsed and immediately regretted, freighted as it was with images of slaughtered horses.

"There's a parallel between my painting and dog food?" growls Simone.

"Imagine this," I am quick to add. "Thousands of gallery- goers coming here to worship a Simone Franklin."

Simone studies my big blues. "You're serious?"

"Very."

"Very scary."

"Not scary. Exciting," I tell her. "Easy."

Simone's eyes travel back to *Sunrise*. "G.B., if it's so easy, tell me why there are no robbers here this very minute."

"What would your usual robber do with a stolen Monet? The thief couldn't ransom it to an insurance company because the Marmottan -- and the usual robber knows this -- the Marmottan can't afford the enormous insurance premiums on its permanent collection." I pause to let that sink in before I continue. "And sell something like *Sunrise* to a private party? How could they show it off to guests? Even to best friends? No, no. Too risky. And French prisons aren't known for their escargots and Pouilly-Fuissé."

"G.B., the thrill machine," Simone sing-songs. "With all your schemes, why aren't you rich?"

"Riches were never my goal. Besides, you have more money than the two of us can ever spend."

Simone raises an eyebrow at me, then turns her attention to the guard, who has just emerged from the water lily room.

"Look at that fox nose and shifty, beady little eyes."

"A no-brainer, that one," I whisper. "Intelligent security guards in museums are about as rare as oceanographers in Afghanistan." My remark falls on deaf ears. Simone's education is sadly lacking in geography, among other things.

"I want to paint him."

"Notice that he is unarmed," I say, nonchalantly.

Simone is squinting at me now, always a sign of great curiosity. "Okay, G.B., out with the master plan."

For that, she gets a loving grin. "Not to worry. Trust me. You paint, I plot."

"But -- "

"For the time being, just think of us as a Ways and Means Committee. I'm the Ways -- "

"And I'm the Means?"

"It could be the greatest spoof of the century!"

Simone gets to her feet and I trail her across the room to *Sunrise*. "Hummm. Wonder what he primed that with."

I can see I've hooked her, and all I have to do now is reel her in. "You can think of it as a little rearrangement of reality," I tell her.

"Commonly known as theft."

"Uncommonly known as a lark." I give her a rare wink. "What do you say we settle down by the Seine for a few months? You paint, I write?"

"Please, you're not really thinking about *The Deposition*? Let sleeping dogs lie."

"How cruelly you put it!" I give her my imitation bloodhound eyes. "All it would need is some cutting and pasting mainly. Think of it as a bit of cosmetic surgery on the face of reality."

"That would amount to a double forgery!"

"A double deposition."

"Plagiarism is a criminal act too, G.B."

"Let's call it mimesis."

"Please, no more extension of my vocabulary today, Professor. My mind is getting ugly stretch marks."

I take Simone's arm. "What do you say we stroll back over to that rental agency in Passy and take the apartment? The one we saw on the Quai des Grands Augustins?"

Simone plants a wet kiss on my neck -- another feature of her exasperating but exciting exhibitionism -- and says, "It does have the biggest bed in all Paris!"

What can I say? Simone was sex-starved when I met her, and sex-starved she still is and probably will always be. And to tell the truth, I like her that way.

CHAPTER TWO

"I could sue you for this!"

My eyes are moist with memories today as I stand in front of the huge picture window in the living room of our Left Bank apartment. From the sixth and top floor at No. 47 on the Quai des Grands Augustins, we overlook the Pont des Arts footbridge over the Seine. Here the river encircles the big island -- the Ile de la Cité -- at the far end of which is Notre Dame Cathedral. At this end is the Pont Neuf -- the oldest bridge in Paris -- and at the tip of the island, the Square du Vert Galant. It's a quiet, triangular park beyond which, on the Right Bank, is the Louvre. Above that, on a clear day, we can see the white domes of the Sacré Coeur Basilica on the distant hill of Montmartre.

"Pumpkin," I call out over my shoulder, "come here?"

Wrapped in a new white terrycloth robe that matches mine, Simone emerges from her studio. She notes the puddles in my big blues and slips an arm around my waist. "What's wrong, Babe?"

I point to the Square. "That's where I used to sit. When the quays belonged to the fishermen and bums and dogs and lovers and loners. Before they turned them into parking lots."

"Yeah," she mumbles.

Yeah? That's all? Proof that Simone has no sense of history. She feels no nostalgia either, unless it's for what never was.

"That was 1965," I say. "Twenty years ago."

"I know the story. You were an escapee from the University of Indiana. On your Junior Year Abroad."

"It really took some tail-cracking to get my parents to agree to letting me go."

"Tail-cracking?"

I chuckle. "Comes from one of the stories I heard at my father's knee. About his boyhood on the prairies and the Great Winter of 1882. They ran out of wood for the fire, burned up all the furniture, and the only way they could get the oxen to plow through the snow to the river where there were trees was to crack their tails. So they'd lurch forward."

Simone emits a sound not unlike the heroine's scream as she leaps from the parapet in the final act of *Tosca*. I have forgotten my audience, I remind myself, and glance covertly at the animal lover at my side. "Well, it's true," I say, and put an apologetic spin on: "It's called survival."

"How could you?" hisses Simone.

How could I what?

Time to change the subject.

I point out the window. "I used to sit right there. Under the arch of the Pont Neuf. Where the guy in a white bikini is standing."

My diversionary tactic works. Simone says, "Looks more like his underwear."

"I'd dangle my Parisian-white legs over the edge of the quay," I go on. "Barefoot in April. I'd look up here and drool over these huge apartment windows full of plants. And dreams."

"He is really odd."

"I remember when lunch was Sorbonne spaghetti smeared with tomato. I must have eaten tons of baguettes. We drank wine in plastic bottles. We all used métro tickets a dozen times each and never got caught. You can't do that anymore with the new machines."

"Look how he's half hiding under the archway there."

Simone presses her nose against the window. "See that lone girl down there wailing away on her saxophone? White underwear is trying to get her attention. See how he's hunching over?"

It looks to me like the underwear is about to hit the cobblestones. "Obviously, he's an exhibitionist," I say.

And obviously, the girl likes what she sees. She places her saxophone in its case and the pair disappear under the arch.

I take advantage of this attention break and ask, "How would you like a peek at something else?"

I take Simone's arm and propel her into my study, which flanks the living room to the east as Simone's does to the west. The kitchen, by the way, is separated from the living room by a wet bar and four stools with padded arms that look like they could hold a drunk in place all evening. Flanking the kitchen on Simone's side are the bedroom and bath, and on my side, the dining room and entryway.

I have furnished my study with a huge oak desk that matches the built-in bookcases, two chocolate-leather armchairs, and a matching couch. It is here that Simone now sprawls, draping one bare leg over the back, suggesting peeks of another kind.

I waive the invitation and hand her the first chapter of *The Deposition.*

"You know," she says, ignoring it, "I've been staring at that reproduction we bought of *Sunrise* all morning. It's a sunset, of course. I mean, even I can figure out that Le Havre faces west."

I tap my manuscript. "Have a look?"

Simone is peering at the wall as if she can see through it. "Looks like Monet did it over something else, like another start, because there's thick impasto in some of the sky areas, like maybe he had scraped down some other painting because some of the impasto areas have thin oil washes over them and much of the painting is thin oil washes and the boat and some of the waves in the front have been put over all the rest with thick impasto again so he laid in the reflections in the water in creams and roses, and then laid in the sky and let it dry, then he went back and added the boats and background garbage."

Simone's tendency to verge on the inarticulate when discussing art has prompted me to give up trying to punctuate such tiring tirades as this. I try to get her back on track with: "We're talking *my* forgery."

I wave the flat of my hand up and down a few times in front of her eyes, and Simone finally picks up my manuscript, which I've printed out on legal paper.

I point to the Table of Contents. "Part I will be the deposition taken by Dorothy Howell. Part II: the deposition taken by Sally S. Smock. Part III: Appendices."

"I can read," she snorts, and together we scan page one:

SUPERIOR COURT OF THE STATE OF CALIFORNIA
IN AND FOR THE COUNTY OF RIVERSIDE

ELLA AGNES GRETCH,   )   *CASE NO. 35890*
     Plaintiff,   )   *PALM SPRINGS*
vs.   )
SIMONE FRANKLIN, et al.,   )
     Defendants.   )
_____)

DEPOSITION OF ELLA AGNES GRETCH
VOLUME I
taken before Dorothy Howell, Shorthand Reporter and a Notary Public in and for the County of Riverside, State of California, commencing at 1:30 p.m., Thursday, February 28, 1984, at the law offices of Bennett, Baines & Bohrman, 4763 Tahquitz Way, Palm Springs, California.

APPEARANCES

FOR THE PLAINTIFF:
CALVIN C. CARNEY
Attorney at Law
31-796 Avenue 44
Indio, California 92201

FOR THE DEFENDANTS:
BENNETT, BAINES & BOHRMAN
Attorneys at Law
By: P. Crawford Bennett
4763 Tahquitz Way
Palm Springs, California 92263
ALSO PRESENT: SIMONE FRANKLIN

Simone erupts with: "You haven't even changed the names, G.B.! The NAMES!"

I shrug. "I'll change them later. Read on?"

"'Ella Agnes Gretch,'" she sing-songs in a three-year-old voice, "'called as a witness on behalf of the defendant, having been first duly sworn by the Notary Public, was examined and testified as follows.' Blah, blah, blah."

"Please? Let's read it?" I begin with Mr. Bennett's first question: "'Would you state your full name for the record?'"

Simone humors me with: "'Ella Agnes Gretch. But most folks call me Aggie.'"

"'Where do you presently reside?'"

"'Box 1470, Indio.'"

I burst out laughing. "She lives in a box! You see? Just giving her address, Aggie is high camp."

Simone gives me not even a wisp of a smile.

I continue: "'Now I won't try to trick you, Mrs. Gretch. If you don't understand the questions, please tell me and I'll try to rephrase them.'"

"'Fair enough.'"

13

"'Do you know of any reason why your deposition can't be taken today? Are you ill or under the influence of medication?'"

"'Well, only that I did have a touch of diarrhea over the week-end, but I guess it's under control now.'"

"'Let's hope so, Mrs. Gretch.'"

With that, Simone crushes the page in her fist and fires it across the room. "Diarrhea, my foot!" she bellows. "That hypochondriac!"

"You're spoiling my narrative line."

"YOUR narrative line?"

I humbly retrieve the mangled page. "Read on?"

"Why should I? I know this trash by heart: December. 1968. The new housekeeper, Ella Agnes Gretch, arrives at Priscilla Franklin's home at 725 Palisades Drive, Palm Springs. Now Aggie can tell Mr. Bennett how she worked her fingers to the bone for Mrs. Franklin and daughter. Cooked, cleaned, gardened, did the pool, did the repairs. 'Managed the whole she-bang' is how Aggie put it. Until the next December, when Mommie Dearest kicked her out."

"You're forgetting an important detail: you were fifteen, Aggie thirty-eight. That sets the stage for more than housework."

Simone gasps. "You're leaving all that in?"

"Of course. Aggie took advantage of a teenager. Some might call that child molesting."

"I can't believe you're spilling my guts all over these pages."

"It's transformed into fiction. It's a novel."

"It's my life!"

"It's both." I tap my manuscript. "Read on? We're coming to Christmas Eve when your mother-- "

"Don't need to." Simone shakes her head. "You think I could ever forget that evening? When she threw Aggie's clothes out in the street?"

"Because your mother was jealous of her?"

"That's what Aggie said."

"But there was more to it than that?"

"I had to call the cops that night because all hell was breaking loose. Mom and her crumbum lover were higher'n kites. Aggie said we'd better get out of there, like now! So I grabbed the keys to Mom's Porsche, and there we were barreling out the driveway with my mother crawling on the hood of the car, loaded to the gills and waving a World War II bayonet Daddy Dearest had dragged home from Germany -- that was before their messy divorce -- and she was screaming at both of us and...." Simone falls suddenly silent.

"So then Aggie got an apartment in Palm Springs," I prompt, pointing to the next page of my *Deposition*.

"This is supposed to be news to me?" snaps Simone. "Aggie telling about her odd jobs? Waitress work? Now you want me to relive my senior year in high school? Go through hell again with my mother? Escape to Aggie's apartment -- "

"Where she manipulated your young mind -- "

"Well, what do you think you're doing right now?"

"Manipulating words."

"What's your point, G.B.?" snarls Simone. "Why do this?"

"Because it's the perfect post-modern novel. You notice that there is no narration in it. It's all dialogue. It's pure Aggie with no commentary. It's up to each reader to interpret her. To write the novel herself."

"Yeah, yeah. All show and no tell. Literature 101. More like Lit Clit 101."

"You're missing the point. I'm telling a story of relationships. Peering beneath the surface of things. Seeing Aggie in a new perspective. Isn't that what all art does? *Sunrise* included."

"Aggie? A piece of art?"

"Also a con artist, yes. She conned you into moving to Los Angeles with her the day after you left high school, didn't she? Right after your mother gave you a new car for graduation?"

"Mom thought I was going alone," mutters Simone. "To go to art school. Dear Dad didn't give a damn, just as long as I didn't appear on his doorstep in Boston."

I tap my manuscript again. "You're getting ahead of yourself."

Simone glances through the remaining pages of my chapter, commenting as she goes: "Those few years in Los Angeles with Aggie were depressing. Got that, G.B.? Me trying to squeeze money out of Mom, living on her credit cards. Aggie supposedly trying to hold a job doing waitress work in all those great celebrity watering holes, like Billy's Lounge, The Flying Tiger Café, Millie's Restaurant on Western -- which burned to the ground one mysterious evening.... The only good part of those years was art school."

"Aren't you leaving out something?" I grin. Then lower my voice to Mr. Bennett's baritone and read from the last page: "'Now Mrs. Gretch, I don't mean to be indelicate, but I do have to find out certain facts. It's my job as a lawyer. Isn't it true that at some point in time you and the defendant became romantically involved with each other?'"

Simone obliges me by delivering the next lines, spoken by Aggie's lawyer Mr. Carney, in his thin tenor voice: "'I instruct the witness not to answer. Irrelevant, immaterial, not likely nor susceptible to lead to relevant and material evidence.'"

I say, "'Mrs. Gretch, are you going to follow your counsel's instruction not to answer the question?'"

Simone gives me an Aggiesque: "'You got that right.'"

"End of chapter," I say. "Well, what do you think?"

"Irrelevant and immaterial!" Simone dramatically rips my page in half, locks eyes with me, and her next comment rattles my teeth: "I could sue you for this!"

"You wouldn't dare."

Would she?

CHAPTER THREE

"Rear End Publications"

Simone has finally calmed down, and I am now curled up on the floor beside the couch -- where she continues to sprawl -- toying with the hem of her robe. She is still toying with after-images inspired by my manuscript.

"You expect your readers to have pity on that old fool?" she mutters. "Aggie has a mind like a flea market. Mostly junk."

I smile, knowing Simone's addiction to garage sales. "Lots of people love flea markets."

"I can't believe you're calling that garbage a novel."

"What's a novel, but an arrangement of reality by words?"

"Is that a quote?"

"I do nothing but quote. Sometimes it's just more obvious."

Simone's eyes close. "This isn't going to work, G.B.," she informs me. "Not your paper, not your caper."

I shake my head, even if she's not looking at me. "As for the manuscript," I tell her, "we're the perfect pair: the omniscient narrator and the omniscient reader."

"You give me no choice."

"As for the heist, we're another perfect pair. Just as a novel has both contents and organization, you create the ingredients for the snatch, and I make the arrangements."

"Look, G.B., you've had a look at my ingredients. Now I want to hear about arrangements. I want details. Details!"

These I have wanted to keep to myself as long as possible, but I can see that I'll lose her at this point if I don't drop a few clues. "You know," I say in hardly more than a whisper, "we're going to need some help with the heist."

"Noooo kidding!"

"Maybe four others. I'm counting on a group called Les Guérillères."

"Les Guérillères?" she mutters. "Are you going to translate or do I haul out my dictionary?"

"The female warriors. They took the name from Monique Wittig's novel," I explain. "But they won't know what I'm really up to."

"Make that five."

"They'll think we're just out to make them notorious."

Simone gives me a Mr. Bennett: "I won't try to trick you."

"They'll want to prove that it's in the interest of the French government to improve the security system at the Marmottan, which is ridiculous. Everybody knows that."

Simone cocks an ear towards the living room. "Are you deaf? The phone's ringing."

I give her my imitation Aggie, "Deaf as I can be and still hear," and trot off.

I am gone no longer than two minutes. But when I walk back into my study, I note that Simone's eyes have taken on an ominous hooded appearance.

"So who are they? Les Guérillères?"

"A feminist group of elite Parisian literati, underground for reasons which will become obvious."

"To who?"

"Whom."

"So whom was on the phone?"

"A gallery owner I talked with the other day. Céline used to go there a lot."

"Céline? Your old love?"

"My old friend."

"Does she have a last name?"

"Chantefable."

"Age?"

"Scars? Tattoos? Birthmarks? Come on, Simone. I told you she was a colleague. And she knows Les Guérrilères. In fact, I suspect that by now she's one of their ring leaders."

"Say what?"

"Like I've told you, I haven't been able to come up with an address or phone number for Céline. But she used to be tight with an artist by name of Pauline Peyre, who used to exhibit at the Galerie Brichant, which is why I went there yesterday. Anyway, Pauline stopped in there this morning, and so the owner gave her my phone number. And now she called back. She wouldn't give me any information about Céline over the phone, but she did agree to meet me."

"And you talk about my tiring tirades!"

"I have a rendezvous with her in an hour. Under Danton's finger."

"What's that supposed to mean?"

"Danton's statue at the Odéon métro stop. Remember? Danton standing there pointing his finger at the sky?"

Simone eyes me with disbelief. "I'm going with you."

"You don't have to bother."

"I am going."

Arguing with Simone is a total waste of time. I have to find other ways to crack her tail. So I say, "Okay, fine. But first I need your input for my novel."

"I gave you the original copy of Aggie's deposition. What more do you want?" Here Simone flashes her wrists at me. "Want me to slit these, too?"

"Actually, I need your approval."

"So I won't sue you?"

"You put it so cruelly."

"Give me one good reason to help you."

"I want to prove that there is no threshold between

19

fiction and non-fiction. That the greatest art is the purest rendition of reality. Actually, that the greatest illusion is reality."

Simone snorts. "So where does that put your love for Monet and Impressionism?"

"It's not Monet, it's you I'm in love with. It's you who are rendering Monet in the purest form. Again, blurring that threshold between illusion and reality."

"We're both nothing but forgers, and you know it."

I shake my head. "We're creative artists."

"Schizophrenics. With multiple personality disorder."

"And I love every one of your personalities," I say, sitting down now on the sliver of couch between Simone's sprawled body and the edge. "You as Micha Markova, leading the Corps de Ballet through *Swan Lake*." Here I let my lips wander from the hem of her terrycloth robe down her right leg, and I nibble a pink bracelet for her ankle.

"Tickles," she murmurs, eyes closed, squirming beneath my crafty kisses.

I smile at her ballerina toes, curled now and pointing towards the stage. "You as Medina, the famous belly dancer-"

"Wish I had never told you about Medina," mutters Simone.

With one finger I push aside her robe, then lean over and place butterfly wing kisses on and about her navel. "You as Kali -- "

"No!" Simone's eyes flare open as she jerks herself up to a sitting position, and in the process flings me to the floor.

"Hey!" I massage the back of my head.

"Don't you ever mention Kali again."

"But -- "

"Is that all you do, G.B.? Expose people's private thoughts? Exhibit their inner feelings for everyone to see?"

"But I -- "

"You do it in your so-called novel just like you do it in reality."

"But I thought we were sharing an intimacy," I say, truly dazed. "And with the novel I thought I was doing you a favor."

"Favor!" she rasps. "You don't publish intimacies!"

"A deposition is not meant to be private. It's a legal record, a public record, to be used in a court of law. Besides, I want the novel to show how Aggie mistreats her Simone."

"I was never HER Simone."

"And how Simone finally realizes what Aggie has been doing to her. How she's been running her life."

"Humph!"

"And how Simone breaks free -- "

"And rushes into the arms of her new lover? Yeah, yeah." Simone pauses to read some invisible writing on the far wall before she says, "I suppose I'm going to have to pay to have that stinkin' thing published for you."

I get to my feet and toss off a flip, "Well, what are multi-millionaires for?" together with an answer: "You can have your very own publishing house: Rear Guard Publications."

"Rear End Publications." Simone's eyes close again. "I feel like getting drunk," she informs me. "How about opening something?"

"Something with a red stripe?" I'm all chirps. "I'm on my way."

For some reason I walk to the kitchen as if I were maneuvering about in a rowboat on a choppy sea, careful not to upset the balance.

From the refrigerator I pull out a bottle of Cordon Rouge and set about removing the foil wrapper from the cork. Then my eyes fall upon the baguette lying on a counter, waiting for dinnertime. A brilliant idea flashes through my mind, inspired no doubt by my recent butterfly wing kisses and the fleshy response they received.

Simone, who has forbidden the use of any sex toys in her presence, nevertheless has a fine sense of humor. How can I resist? I take a bread knife, slice the baguette in half, and conceal -- rounded end down -- one crusty foot-long piece beneath my terrycloth robe. Grasping the belt with one hand, I gingerly hold it in place. I slip the fingers of my other hand around the stems of two champagne flutes, then grasp the bottle of Cordon Rouge and do a hidden-baguette shuffle back into my studio.

Simone is posing now, half-reclining against pillows, half-smiling, waiting for coming attractions.

"G.B., what are you up to now?" She studies my big blues. "Something weird is going on in that mad mind of yours."

I wave the Cordon Rouge up and down a few times. "Just a bit of the bubbly and...SURPRISE!"

One little jerk on my belt and my robe falls open to expose the perfectly-positioned half-baguette, which rises magically to the occasion. At the same time my shaken bottle of champagne does not wait for me to pull its plug, and the exploded cork shatters the plaster overhead while froth and foam spew forth onto my now hysterical Simone, whose screams reverberate over the rooftops of Paris.

I cannot remember to this day what happened next.

According to Simone, she grabbed my baguette and whacked me over the head with it until we both finally collapsed in laughter. Then we began guzzling the bubbly straight from the bottle, slurping up the surplus where it fell. As for the baguette, I do remember finding its mangled remains the next day, crammed under a pillow, chewed at both ends and limp in the middle, and don't ask me how or why.

CHAPTER FOUR

"Deaf as you can be and still hear."

It is the following afternoon, and I push back from my desk, satisfied with my day's work. Simone, too, has seemed pleased with hers. I know, because I've played Peeping Tom from time to time, spying on her through a generous keyhole as she mixed colors on her palette and delicately applied them to her canvas. Poetry in motion: no other words for my Claudia Monet.

I prop my bare feet up on my desk and congratulate myself. Everything is on target: the novel, the painting, the heist. This latter got a push yesterday -- after the baguette affair -- under Danton's finger, where I charmed Céline's phone number out of Pauline Peyre, leading me one step closer to the Guérillères. And to the caper of capers.

What do I see appearing now in my doorway but my artist. She gets a big time smile from me as I appraise her costume: a frilly white blouse tucked into skin-tight mustard-suede pants with stiletto boots to match. And golden earrings as large as onion rings, perhaps inspired by the old Marlene Dietrich film we caught on TV last night.

"I have a treat for you," I tell her seductively. "I phoned Céline's number again a little while ago and finally got her familiar voice instead of her answering machine!"

Simone flops into one of my armchairs and smirks, "Trick or treat?"

"Céline has to be one of the most utterly sparkling intellects in all France. She has read everybody. Met everybody."

"Knows everything."

"She agreed to have dinner with us tonight. So I told her I'd call her back after I'd checked with you."

Simone yawns. "I feel like slumming tonight."

"Then I'll tell her we'll meet at La Mangerie. If Aggie had been a Parisian, she surely would have worked there."

"Billy's Lounge and the Flying Tiger all rolled into one?"

"With a French twist."

I gather the chapter I have just completed and hand it to Simone. "Now for my second treat."

"Yuk," she mutters, but accepts the pages, which I read with her, over her shoulder:

BY MR. BENNETT: Let's go back on the record.

Q. Mrs. Gretch, you say you were sick a good deal that winter. What was your problem?

A. I had another problem, that I could not hear at all. I was totally deaf as you can be and still hear.

Q. I see. Now the following spring, did Mrs. Franklin ask Simone to go with her to Europe?

A. Actually, Simone was scared to get overseas and then if her mother went out carousing and got drunk and passed out or whatever, well, Simone just plain panicked. So I told her she should tell her mother that she had this dream that they were both on an airplane and it crashed. And Simone did. And that sure terminated Priscilla's thoughts on going to Europe.

Simone stares at the ceiling and mumbles something incoherent.

"While you read on," I say, "I'll phone Céline. And since it's almost the cocktail hour, why don't I also pour us a little libation?"

Silent Simone is still staring at the ceiling as I head for the kitchen.

I am in the process of removing the cork from a bottle of Mumm's when Simone calls out, "Can you hear me?"

I call back, "I'm deaf as I can be and still hear," and begin filling two antique Venetian flutes that Simone recently purchased for as many francs as I used to live on for a month in my student days here.

Her "Screw you!" momentarily stops my hand in mid-air. But I finish pouring the champagne and waltz back into my studio and offer Simone an icy flute.

In exchange, she offers me a fistful of pages. "You think I need to read about my mother's death?" she snarls. "Like I'm short on memories?"

"The reader needs to know that when she died -- "

"May 31, 1972."

" -- that you and Aggie left Los Angeles and moved to the Palisades house in Palm Springs."

"And lived there unhappily ever after. Until November of 1983, that is."

"And that during those approximately twelve years Aggie was not employed."

Simone closes her eyes and in a voice eerily like Aggie's, hoarse with years of puffing on Marlboros, says: "Mr. Bennett, I didn't have time for any other jobs. I hardly had time to do what I did when I did it, which Simone used to be upset about."

Not to be upstaged, I continue the ad lib scene in my Mr. Bennett baritone: "But at some point Simone suggested that you apply for disability?"

"Pardon me?"

"Okay, it's like pulling teeth in here today, I tell you. Mrs. Gretch, what did you tell social security?"

"I didn't tell them that I was unable to work or the reason that I had talked with social security was that I had an eye problem and so forth, being partially blind, which Simone knew, and, you know, I had been since '70, that I might be able to be compensated for that, which of course did not happen."

"At that time you told the authorities for how long you were disabled and unable to work?"

"I worked for Simone eight to eighteen hours a day, every day, for twelve years, at home and at the rentals, doing all the gardening, the electrical, the plumbing, the painting, why I'd say, Simone, Baby, look, we got to take care of so and so and so and she would say, well, go take care of it, Aggie, you know I don't want to be bothered with that."

With that, Simone fires my manuscript onto my desk, and waves of it splash over onto the carpet. "This is ridiculous! Who's going to care about Aggie?"

"Any feeling person," I answer, patiently gathering up my pages while Simone slumps in her chair and guzzles champagne. "Aggie stirs emotions in you. That's what a novel should do."

"Don't you get it?" Simone's voice has shot up an octave. "I've had enough of Aggie! I gave her everything. Food, lodging, clothing, you name it. I paid for everything. Gave her cash, too." Simone lurches to her feet. "What do you think you're doing, G.B.? You putting me on trial here?"

I can see I've gone too far for one day. "It's Aggie who's on trial here," I say reassuringly. "And it's Simone who's being taken out to dinner. To the restaurant of her choice. By someone who admires and respects her. Delight of my life, that's what I should call you from now on. Delight."

Delight shrugs. "Hummph."

I step to her side and touch my flute to hers. "Dindin? Yes?" I rarely stoop to tinytot talk such as this, but hey, whatever works. It's always a clincher to mellow out Simone. Time to whisper in her ear: "Numnums? Nummynums?"

Simone turns her head and we are now nose to nose. Her "Kisskiss?" is barely breathed.

I take advantage of her parted lips to slip my tongue into her open invitation and penetrate the mysterious organ that deserves a more poetic name than speech.

What a piece of work, the tongue! It may be likened by the aesthetically challenged to the pin of a buckle, to the flap of a shoe, the pole of a wagon, the clapper of a bell. But to one versed in the art of love it is a most precious projection, the cause of effects so startling, so engulfing, that they defy description in the so-called real world of space and time.

Tongue-tied now in our own sweet seamless world, our mouths make of verbal communication an incidental function, and of love a melody we go on humming long after the show is over.

CHAPTER FIVE

"Olga Tchika-Tchikaboomskaya!"

It is sheer nostalgia that guides my footsteps this evening, given the incredible variety of eateries within walking distance from our apartment. You can taste anything from Pizza Pino in a sidewalk café to Canard à l'orange on the top floor of the Tour d'Argent where, by the way, Simone dropped $400 plus tip for dinner for the two of us last week.

You want sushi? You can have sushi. Tapas? Eat tapas. Thai, Russian, Vietnamese, Peruvian? You got it. And there's Greek food galore, especially in the Latin Quarter, where you can eye every shishkebob and fishkebob and spitted pig -- and Simone does just that -- before choosing just the right one for your Aegean orgy. There's even a salad bar in the Rue Gregoire de Tours, favored by look-alike American coeds putting in their Junior Year Abroad. Whether from Bryn Mawr or Brown, Scripps or Swarthmore, they're all on diets and all putting on weight. It's the pâtisseries that do them in.

En route to La Mangerie this evening to meet Céline, Simone and I pause in the Place Saint-Germain-des-Prés for the street entertainment: two flamenco dancers, one fire-eater, and a Cityrama bus filled with tourists whose heads move in military cadence -- left, right, left, right -- to microphoned messages.

Then we spot the bag lady in black rubber boots. ("They all wear black rubber boots. That's how you can tell them." So saith Simone.) After rifling through a trash container on the corner, the woman turns to stick her dark tongue out at a group of *apéritif* sippers on the sidewalk of the Café aux Deux Magots. Simone cheers her on with a, "Yeeesss!"

Simone, I regret to say, has never shown any appreciation for the Deux Magots, one of the most celebrated cafés in Paris to which the expatriate existentialist needs no introduction. It was there, from the late forties to the early sixties, before groups of admiring disciples, that Jean-Paul Sartre and Simone de Beauvoir exchanged existential anguish on a regular basis. I, in fact, had the intense pleasure one evening of eavesdropping on one of their last café conversations.

A stone's throw away from the Deux Magots, in the short, narrow Rue des Cannettes, is the miniature La Mangerie. Once through the tiny doorway -- reminiscent of 11th century castles built for people who were tall at five feet -- we can see little with our murky champagne vision but the low ceiling. From it, two-by-twos are suspended to hold the baguettes, which rest perpendicularly on the boards. Simone eyes them, has instant flashback, and pokes a wanton elbow in my ribs.

Above the hum of smoky conversations we can hear a guitarist in the dimmer recesses. I peer about for a glimpse of Céline, but we are a bit early and she is nowhere in sight.

A lilting "*Bonsoir!*" comes from our waiter-to-be who seats us at one of the tipsy little wooden tables lighted by dime store candles. With his head bandanaed, ears earringed, neck and waist scarved, extremities jingling-jangling with trinkets, he is instantly dubbed by Simone as Olga Tchicka-Tchicka*boom*skaya!

"What are people drinking in those, Olga?" she wants to know, hooking a thumb towards two glasses on a nearby table.

"House rotgut," I tell her.

"I'll have one."

"From Mumm to bum?"

Simone holds up two fingers to Olga and nods towards the two glasses. Then fastforwards with: "What do we eat, G.B.? Shareseys?"

I instantly regret my own tinytot talk earlier this evening which has probably inspired more of same, often embarrassing, especially here in public.

"We have a dinner guest," I remind her. "And politeness dictates that we wait for said guest before ordering."

"I'm starving!"

I wave my hands in the air to signify there's nothing to do but wait. At the same time I pick up a more adult conversation from a corner table. It's not long before Simone is at me with, "You're eavesdropping on that couple."

"What couple?" I ask, as if she's hallucinating the pair.

"That old professor-pushing-sixty type and his young chick, probably a grad student writing a dissertation that has a title half a page long and four volumes of bibliography."

"They're discussing Jacques Derrida's brilliant novel, *Glas*. Based on his philosophy of deconstruction -- "

"Is it in French or gobbledegook?"

According to Simone, gobbledegook is the language in which all post-structuralist literary criticism is written.

"Speak!" Simone utters this to me as if she were commanding a dog.

"I'd say they're having a core conversation," I tell her nonchalantly. "They're arguing the question of whether or not matter is, in fact, an epiphenomenon of mind."

Simone slurps the wine Olga has just served us. "You've got to be kidding."

I have reached a two-can-play-this-game attitude and respond with a cool, "Why?"

"In a candlelit restaurant at eleven o'clock at night?" Simone shoves down into her seat and mad-dogs the couple. "You'd rather be sitting with them, wouldn't you?"

"Don't be silly."

"Is that what you and your Sorbonne lover used to discuss here?"

I fold my arms, ready for battle. "She did mention an orthogonal view of the universe from time to time."

"Orthogonal? That must be a reference to a mattress."

"You're getting out of hand, Simone."

"This rotgut is getting better by the inch. Look at the patterns in it. That's the universe for you. All patterns. Women: the great pattern makers. Not to be confused with these new feminist quilters. The great pattern makers sitting around on their fat asses making Nothing New quilts. Reduced to *that!* Burns the shit out of me! Ask Olga for another glass of rotgut, will you?"

"Could you please keep it down a little?"

"Olga?" This she calls out, of course.

Our waiter jingle-bells over.

I try to maintain control by telling him, "*Encore deux, s'il vous plaît.*"

Simone upstages me with, "More rotgut, *s'il vous plaît.*"

Olga winks at us again and jangles off.

Simone rants on: "Life. It's all patterns. Just find the pattern and everything else falls into place. One of these days I'll come up with your pattern too, G.B. Then I'll be on to you just like I'm on to your hero Sartre and his tacky little existential novel."

"Sartre? Tacky? Really, Simone. Sartre is a monument to twentieth-century thought."

"Make that nineteenth century."

One thing I have to say about Simone: she never forgets a thing she learns. And she puts it all together in her own inimitable way. Nevertheless, I give her an argumentative, "What gives you the right to make such statements?"

"According to you, no one can think, no one can understand, no one has a right to say anything without a

31

fuckin' Ph.D. Or two. Two is better yet."

"Two *are* better," I say quietly as Olga sets two fresh glasses of wine on our table.

In the interest of keeping Simone as sober as possible, I bypass the etiquette called for this evening and ask Olga for one order of mussels in garlic mayonnaise, one of steak tartare, and an extra plate. He winks and swivels away.

Meanwhile, my grammatical correction has put Simone into a silent sulk. Good. I need a break from her sudden streak of foul language. Sometimes I think she has Tourette Syndrome. And if you think her 'is' is bad, you should have witnessed her appalling grammar when I first met her. That meeting, by the way, took place at the Hilton Hotel in Palm Springs at an enormous women-only party that supposedly celebrated both the Dinah Shore golf tournament and Spring Break. I went down from the University of California at Santa Barbara, where I had been a poorly-paid Ph.D. long enough to reach burn-out stage.

Simone still doesn't know it, but I don't have a Ph.D. The University of California doesn't know it either. My résumé states that I attended the Sorbonne for a year and received a B.A. from the University of Indiana. This is true. It also indicates that I did a Master's Degree at Northwestern in comparative literature. This also is true. But by then my family was dead, and I had blown my meager inheritance on a Jaguar. And I needed a change.

For awhile I wrote theses for students who were long on bucks and short on brains. That bought me an IBM 360 that kept me financially afloat and intellectually amused for a few more years, but I eventually drowned in the mediocrity of it all. By then I was long on computer tricks and short on larks. I decided to tack a Ph.D. on to my résumé -- in the privacy of my own home.

The transcript I came up with from the University of Chicago was a smasher! Grad course titles that would make your head spin, and A's for every one except "Theoretical

Spectroscopy and Derridian *différence*: Reinterpreting Phenomenology." For this I gave myself an A minus together with an explanation for the interrogation committee at UCSB, where I had applied for a position.

"It was due to something more than a personality clash between Professor Booth and me," I told them with a scholarly frown. "We differed totally regarding the role of women in phenomenological theory."

The committee agreed with me that my opposing views would lend spice and stimulation to the Women's Studies seminar scheduled for their new assistant professor. I chewed my bottom lip bloody to keep from laughing.

The committee members were also ridiculously impressed with my dissertation which, I admit, took me a good six months to write. I also admit that it was a challenge getting it through the Library of Congress and on microfilm and available to any gullible student or professor in any university library. But it was all a harmless caper. Another Ken-L-Ration substitution in the steak and kidney pie. If the consumer can't tell the products apart, what's the difference?

Nevertheless, you can imagine how tiresome all of the above became. And how I was yearning for a far wilder caper by the time I met my soulmate, Simone.

She is now staring at me defiantly as Olga delivers our mussels and steak tartare. She waves the wine glass that she has just emptied with one great gulp and hands it to Olga for a refill. Clearly, my plot and subplot are both heading for the rocks.

"Please, Simone."

"Why do you put up with me?"

"You fascinate me," I tell her truthfully. "But tell me why you put up with me?"

Simone answers questions only when she damned well pleases. She stays on the attack with, "So you find ignorance fascinating?"

"You're more than ignorant -- "

Simone sticks her tongue out at me just like the bag lady at the Deux Magots. "What an icky intellectual remark."

"Icky?" Her vocabulary is littered with junk words such as icky. It used to be as appalling as her grammar.

"You are so full of intellectual bullshit!" Simone slams her fist down on our wobbly table and the dime store candle does a pirouette. "If only you'd practice what you preach, you'd be writing great original novels."

"And *The Deposition*?"

"It's a fake and you know it."

"Not entirely."

"Close enough."

"You're eating my half of the steak tartare."

Simone gives the plate a shove in my direction. "Here. Eat."

I shove it back. "Never mind. I'll order another."

"And another wine." Simone pauses only long enough to breathe. "You're trying to make a fake out of me, too."

"Oh, come on."

"You're hung up on fakes. Like Sartre. He's so wrapped up in himself that he doesn't really know anybody else exists."

"True, he does make something of a metonymical error in substituting his experiences for Everyman's."

"Everyman? You sexist!"

"I'm quoting."

"Sartre is the whole fake culture. House of cards. Time to leave it behind. Along with all the quilting crap."

"What's beyond quilting?" I ask, admittedly rather mesmerized by her unique train of thought. "Doris Lessing?"

"Screw Doris Lessing and her female quest novels too. Chewing yesterday's garbage. Now women can repeat all men's stupidities. Chewing, chewing. What I want to see are some real radicals. Real changes, all across the board."

"You'll meet a real radical when Céline gets here," I

say, hoping at this point that she won't show up tonight. "Now can we stop arguing?"

"Why should we stop?"

This is my chance, and I seize it. "Because we're two sides of the same coin. Complementary opposites. That's why we belong together. And arguments, resolved, fit us back together again. Each single argument in isolation is invalid."

"Separated, we make two half forgeries?"

"Together a single hoax."

"Patterns Plan. That's where it's at."

"I'm listening."

"See, each concept broken down will give a pattern and each pattern an insight and all insights fed into a computer will give a pattern to save the world."

"From what? Transcendental signifiers?" The moment I say this I know it's a mistake.

"Don't give me that semiological shit!" Simone accompanies this with her left middle finger thrust high over our table.

I glance about the room and groan. "Please -- "

"The computer program to save humanity. Part of Patterns Plan. Redirected quilting. A completed quilt made of new concepts. No, new images. They're what shape lifestyles, not concepts."

I have to agree.

"Ask Olga for another glass of wine, will you? Or I can. Olga?"

By this time I've given up on Céline making an appearance and say, "Simone, let's go home."

"Don't want to go home."

"Simone, I beg you."

"Crude Simone. That's what you're thinking, aren't you?"

"I'm just thinking that you've had too much wine."

"Think I'm turning into an alcoholic like Mommie Dearest?"

"No such thing. Please, Simone? Peace? Reconciliation of opposites? Bed? Beddybye?"

She is slow to affirm the obvious: "I don't know if I can walk."

I am about to offer her my arm when my peripheral vision picks up a pair of women entering La Mangerie. I cannot help but gasp.

Simone's eyes trail mine to the doorway. "Don't tell me," she groans. "Céline? And who's Casper-the-ghost with her? My gawd my gawd my gawd!" With that, Simone wraps her arms around herself and rocks back and forth like an autistic child. "Aggie," she moans. "Aggie, help! Aggieeee!"

CHAPTER SIX

"Forever."

Against my better judgment, Simone has dragged me back to the Marmottan today. It doesn't take a genius to realize that the less they see of us here the better. But after last night, I had no choice. At least we're fairly inconspicuous -- Simone in jeans and the green cashmere turtleneck sweater I gave her last Saint Patrick's Day, and I in jeans pants, shirt, and jacket.

"Today it's my call," she announced this morning, with an ice pack draped over her hangover eyes. "No painting, no heist. No deal. Right?"

I didn't have to think that one over. "Right."

"How could you, G.B.? Bring that twitty professor into our caper, along with her medieval moll? THEY are pulling the heist with us? Give me a break!"

"They may be short on brawn, but they're long on brains." I tapped my cranium. "That's what makes for success."

Simone blew a puff of hot air my way to signify that my remarks were not worth listening to.

I lashed out with, "Well, what did you expect? A couple of diesel dykes?"

Her answer was another puff of hot air. I left her alone in the bedroom and sought sanctuary in my studio.

Last night was messy, to say the least. Céline's excuses for her late arrival with Countess Claire Navret didn't help, either.

"The Countess had a mishap," she explained. "She tripped over a hanger in her closet, fell and hurt her hip."

That sent Simone into a fit of garbled hysteria. "Countesss? Clossset? Hhhanger? Tripppppped?"

After that, it took my verbal acrobatics to keep Simone from ripping Céline and the Countess apart limb from labile limb. Needless to say, they were aghast. I had to convince them that Simone was not at all herself and that her abominable behavior was actually caused by Céline's resemblance to Simone's favorite aunt who had recently died, leaving a black hole in her psyche -- a twisty story I forged in a nanosecond to save both my plot and characters, so to speak.

"You're a fake, G.B.!" is all Simone would say when we got home.

But this morning she had everything to say. She referred to Céline as "That twit in tweeds."

I protested with: "Fashionable tweeds."

"That three-piece vested salt and pepper suit that just matched her hair? Must have bought it in a boys' department. Men's suits don't come that small."

"So?"

"Colorless face," Simone ranted on. "Colorless glasses. Even colorless moles. Eyebrows *au naturel*. Ick! And yapping all the time. Barking off at the mouth."

"You're speaking of one of the most utterly sparkling intellects in all France."

"And those beady little eyes! And that hands-in-pockets swagger!"

"Unkind and unfair."

"And then there's her '*co-vivante*' as she put it. Do they blend! Colorless Countess Claire. With her little French bun of what was once blond hair, I suppose. And that transparent skin that's barely covering her ivory bones. Tacky ivory bracelet -- "

"A priceless heirloom."

"Another bone. To go with that hawk nose, those thin, hawk's-wing eyebrows. And wearing some colorless '40s dress to match the rest of her.

"Chiffon?"

"Something limp, anyway," smirked Simone. "And various and asundry necklaces."

"Various and sundry."

"That huge kidney-stone yellow ring on her finger, falling off the bone -- "

"But what aristocratic cheekbones!"

"Aristocratic, shit! And she had to wear six-inch spike heels -- as if she weren't six feet tall to begin with. All calculated to look down at us with her droopy camel eyes. And that starved-to-death stare to boot. You know, she didn't have to escape from that World War II Lithuanian camp she babbled on about. They would have left her for dead anyway."

"Simone, really."

"Bet she's had at least three eye jobs. Plus a complete body job to wire the old royal bones together. All the better to tell us just how much she has suffered. Singing of her sorrows, seventy-seven swan songs, all in the same key. Suffered, suffered, suffered. And is still suffering. And will continue to suffer."

"Forever," I couldn't help but murmur.

"One thing's for sure, the Countess doesn't have to worry about cooking. She can live on intravenous -- "

I threw up my hands in disgust. "Simone, you have gone beyond simple vulgarity."

"Céline and the Countess, what a pair of dogs! A hyper chihuahua chasing after a half-dazed greyhound!"

I didn't smile, even though her description was as amusing as it was graphically correct. "Your choice of words disgusts me," I told her instead. "Just as it did last night."

"It's all your fault, G.B. You taught me everything I know. In fact, the very first thing I learned from you -- in

Latin, that is -- was *Carpe diem*."

"But as we were saying goodby, did you have to let fly to everyone in the Mangerie your linguistic concoction -- "

"*Carpe noche?*" Simone burst out laughing. "That really sent the dogs yapping."

And her flip reaction sent me into a verbal race-car attack. But I hadn't even had time to shift out of first gear when Simone gave me her hell's-freezing-over look that always says, "I'm shutting down." And when Simone shuts down, it takes a blast of nuclear energy to start her up again. So I capitulated. Or, rather, gave her that impression. After all, I had won a major battle: in spite of her bitter complaints, she had not refused to continue the project with Céline and the Countess.

As Simone and I sit alone now on a bench facing *Impression, Sunrise*, I know that my strategy must take a different tack. If the caper's going to work, I'll have to keep her away as much as possible from the dogs, as she now constantly refers to our future cohorts. Divide and conquer. Or forget it.

Before she can launch more vile comments about them, I tell Simone *sotto voce*, "We'll duplicate the frame too. Take a good look at it."

"Tacky. All the frames down here are alike anyway."

"No problem?"

Simone shakes her head no. "I suppose we're pulling this heist some dark midnight?" she wonders, eyebrows arched.

"Wrong. The security system is operating during the hours the museum is closed. But the alarm system isn't plugged in during visiting hours."

"Give me a break!"

I note that Simone is squinting at me just like she does at *Sunrise*. Probably trying to determine how I turned out the way I did, too. Also wondering if I'm for real. Time to throw her a few more bones.

"It's true. Tourists were always setting off the alarm. Inadvertently, of course."

"So it operates only after hours?"

"Trust me."

"That's ridiculous!"

"Want to try it?"

"No!"

I glance through the doorway and note that both the downstairs guards have come together in the next room and are deep in conversation. "Well then I'll try it," I tell Simone. "Come on into the corner here. See? You can jiggle the painting, pull on the cords, and nothing."

Simone takes a while to process that revealing bit of information before she backtracks and says, "So when, then?"

"On a Sunday morning. Fewer tourists."

With that, I take her arm and escort her upstairs and outside and hail a passing taxi. Just after we cross the Seine over to the Left Bank, I spot a shop with an awning lettered *QUINCAILLERIE*. "Stop here," I tell the driver, and to Simone I say, "I'll be just a couple of minutes."

She shrugs, and I pop out of the taxi and into the hardware store. There I draw a sketch for the clerk and explain how I want to hang a board about a meter square parallel with a ceiling. I ask for a roll of wire and four hooks that would do the job. He says nothing as he prepares a package for me, but his eyes tell me I could use some professional help -- the psychiatric kind.

As we are driven back to our apartment, Simone of course plagues me with whispered questions, which I cooly ignore. But as soon as we are safely inside our living room, I let her know that I can rant and rave, too.

"You want to ruin this caper?" I yell. "What makes you think the driver didn't understand English? What makes you think he won't remember us later on, when the Marmottan heist hits the papers? My God, Simone, you're going to blow the whole thing!"

Her eyes downcast, a meek Simone plops onto the living room couch and mumbles, "I'm sorry."

"You should be!"

"But can't you even tell me what you bought in that shop?"

I open my package for her to see and appreciate. "*Sunrise* on the ceiling? Yes?"

"That's why you borrowed a ladder from the concièrge today?"

"Also a screwdriver and a drill."

Simone sighs and holds out her arms. "Love me?"

"Do YOU love ME? is the question."

"Come here. I'll show you."

"Just answer the question, Mrs. Gretch."

"Yes, Mr. Bennett. Yes."

"How much?"

"Ask and you shall receive."

"Then how about reading my next chapter while I tackle the ceiling?"

Determined to make the most of the moment, I hurry into my study and return with several pages of manuscript. Simone moans when I hand them to her, but as I collect the ladder and tools stashed in the entryway and proceed with them into the bedroom, she is right behind me, obediently scanning the first page.

"You had to tell how my mother's estate was distributed to me?" she squawks. "That I got a fourth of the loot when I was twenty-one and the rest when I was thirty?"

"The reader needs to know," I answer, setting the ladder up at the foot of the bed. "Your mother probably hoped you'd be rid of Aggie by the time you were thirty."

"January of last year. And she was right."

"You see?" I get a yardstick out of the closet and a pencil out of the dresser and mount the ladder. "I came along just in time. If Aggie had still been with you last January, and you had...shall we say...some terrible accident, Aggie would be a multi-millionaire today."

Simone kicks off her pumps and stretches out on the bed, leaning against a pile of pillows. She squints up at me and says, "And guess who would become a multi-millionaire today if I were to drown in the Seine? Or disappear in some back alley of the Flea Market?"

I look down at her and narrow my eyes like Jack Nicholson in some thriller we saw on TV the other night. With thin lips barely parted I say, "Or be smothered with a pillow?" I begin coming down the ladder towards her, slowly, my throat clotted with wicked laughter.

Simone screams. "You stay away from me, G.B.!"

"Enough already!" I mount the ladder again, this time to the top step, and begin measuring for my hooks. "Finish my chapter."

"That wasn't amusing."

Simone takes a good long look at me, then refocuses on my manuscript. "Yuk!" is her next comment. "Now we get the so- called 'oral agreement'?"

"Want to read it to me? I believe Mr. Bennett's question goes something like: Now, Mrs. Gretch, in your complaint you allege that on May 20, 1983, you and Simone entered into an oral agreement whereby plaintiff was allowed to live at the residence. I want to know who witnessed this oral agreement?"

Simone's reading is all imitation Aggie: "'Simone and I.'"

I ad lib Mr. Bennett: "And what were the terms?"

"'We were having a friendly conversation, and I had suggested to her, well, I was to do something about earning money and having an income and so forth, and she said, well, you know Aggie, when we get this estate thing all together and settled, then we'll, well, I'll reimburse you.'"

"Mrs. Gretch, just give me the terms of the agreement."

"'That I would continue working for her rather than

going out and getting a job.'" Simone looks up at me. "What a crock!"

I point to the ceiling and the four dots I've marked for hooks. "That look about right?"

She nods distractedly. "Umhum."

I go down the ladder for the drill and prompt her with another ad-lib Mr. Bennett question: "How much were you to be paid, Mrs. Gretch?"

Simone continues reading: "'I suppose plenty.'"

"Don't tell me what you suppose. How much did you ask her for and how much did she agree to pay?"

"'It had come up about me not having any money. And I said, Simone, you know we are going to have to make some arrangement I guess about what we are going into in this new phase, and so forth, and you know I don't remember the exact wording, how can I remember the exact words?'"

"You're the one that alleged you had an oral agreement," I chuckle. "I want to know what it was."

"'I'm trying to be honest, Mr. Bennett, and say exactly what I said. I don't remember exactly what I said. We were sitting there having coffee and talking about her financial arrangements and so forth and it brought up mine, that I didn't have any money, and that's when she said, Aggie, I don't know how in the hell you're going to work, we have so much to do now, I just don't know when you'd put the time in.'" At the sound of my drill, Simone looks up at me and bursts out laughing. "That's not how you make a hole in the ceiling!"

I pay no attention and continue drilling. Snowflakes of plaster fill the air and soon my eyes, too, and Simone roars as I put the drill down, blind now and coughing as well.

"Aggie could have had ten paintings hung by now," she says.

I rub my eyes. "Not if she had hanged you first," I snarl.

"You got Aggie all wrong, G.B."

"Just finish the chapter? Okay?"

Simone's eyes drift back to the manuscript. "'Well, Mr. Bennett, you ask about our oral agreement, just how long I was to be allowed to live at the residence on Palisades Drive? Well, it was agreed that I would live there if you call that having an agreement, I mean, I was there and had been since Priscilla's passing, and before either Simone was living with me or I was living with her because of the fact that we had, that was what we were doing.'"

"All right, all right. Just tell me how long you were to be allowed to live at the residence?"

"'How long?'"

"How long?"

Almost inaudibly, Simone mutters, "'Forever.'"

I am cautiously silent, never knowing what to expect next. Laughter? Tears? Rage? An outpouring of Tourette Syndrome? Simone is the only person I've ever known who is totally unpredictable. Perhaps that's why I loved her so.

She looks up at me with eyes as forlorn as they are fearful. "You're right," she tells me in nothing more than a whisper. "Aggie really is a pathetic creature. I read this, and even I am beginning to feel sorry for her."

"There! You see?" I screw a hook into the first hole I've drilled. "She is a marvelous character for a novel. She's earthy. She's cunning. She's clever -- "

"She could hang a screen door, fix a toilet -- "

"Nail down a shingle -- "

"Put in a window -- "

"Yes, yes, yes," I chuckle. "And much much more."

As I come down the ladder, Simone is staring blandly at me in a manner I am helpless to interpret. This is a new look. She could be sitting in Afghanistan, she is that far away.

Finally she says, "So, G.B., maybe your novel will be published after all. Maybe I will paint you a great *Sunrise*. And maybe your heist will go off without a hitch. And then what?

Do we live happily ever after?"

    I go over to her and place a slow kiss between her breasts and whisper, "Forever."

CHAPTER SEVEN

"The clothes I had on, and three dogs."

"Zis zsucks!" Simone hurls my latest chapter at the front door of the apartment just as I'm walking in, and the pages splatter my face. "You know vat Gretch rhymes viss?" she snarls, and I detect the odd German accent that now and then creeps into her speech.

"Wretch? Retch?" I offer, and begin retrieving the scrambled papers at my feet, as is now my humble habit.

"I haf to reliff all dis? Zat Sanksgivinghk?"

"What's wrong now?"

Simone goosesteps across the living room. "You vill pay."

I shake my head as I realize once again how damaged she really is. This scenario brings to mind her pathetic stories of childhood. Of visits from Mommie Dearest's brother: Uncle Horst from Hamburg. He would bounce baby on his knee and whisper sweet Faustian nothings in her ear. Simone has since relegated their relationship to a lower floor of her subconscious that her conscious elevator rarely visits. But one day recently when it did make a brief stop at Uncle's floor, Simone saw him winking at her as he peed in Priscilla's rose garden. He called that their secret abracadabra. God knows what other magic tricks he pulled.

Simone rides memories such as this like a rubber raft rides white water. So far she hasn't flipped over, and I have to make sure she doesn't. My job is to put the fun in

47

dysfunctional.

I trail Simone into her studio, the disaster area of our apartment. It's an incredible mess of brushes, paints, canvases, scattered books, magazine clippings, a paint-splattered easel, laundry that never made it to a hamper, and shoes that never made it to a closet.

"You know," I say calmly, "it's good to review the past -- any shrink will tell you that."

"Fuckov!"

"Verbalize it, get it out where you can deal with it."

"YOU deal with it."

I am happy to hear that the German accent is on the wane. "As I used to tell my students, repression equals depression."

Simone's "Humph!" is curt but encouraging.

"You don't keep your wings folded if you want to fly."

"And you don't hang out with turkeys either," mutters Simone.

"Your happiness -- and mine, of course -- is all I really care about. Our life together. Being happy."

"Humph!"

"*The Deposition* should be good for both of us. For me, a literary challenge -- "

"Ha! About as challenging as cribbing answers from your palm on a multiple-choice exam."

I ignore the interruption and say, "For you, a healing process, an awakening -- "

"You got that right. I feel like I've been half asleep most of my life! Watch out when I wake up, G.B.!"

I pause while we both shift gears. "I missed you this evening." This I say as if I were talking to a normal person in normal circumstances. "You really should have come along. When Céline opened her door, I was speechless. Her living room was a disaster area not even you could imagine." Here Simone mimes a Gestapo 'fuckov' before she turns away and goosesteps over to her easel.

I realize my *faux pas* and hurry to cover it with: "Walls stacked with humongous paintings. Now I'm talking weird stuff. Ghoulish birdwomen, five star nightmare variety, really gutsy. And there stands Céline, a huge wooden noodle fork in one hand, and back through a doorway I see a long wooden table. Big bowl of noodles on it. Candles burning. And guess who? Countess Claire!"

Simone whirls around and flings a paintbrush my way. I grab it in mid-air. It is sticky with cerulean blue, and now my fingers are, too. I march over to her easel and slam the paintbrush in the tray. Simone wants drama, I'll give her drama alright. We'll see who's in charge here.

"Enough of this childishness," I snap.

"Listen up, G.B. You have one fatal flaw. You either underestimate people or overestimate them."

"Okay, Simone, now you listen up! I'm giving you a chance at the caper of the century, and what do you do? Show enthusiasm? No. Appreciation? No. No nothing. Dammit, I'm tired of trying to please you. You hear me?"

"I hear you. And what's more, I'm out of this whole crazy scheme. You know, if you had suggested hiring a few thugs to work with us, I'd have believed in you. But those dogs? Come on, G.B., out with it. What's really going on? You owe me that much."

I remove a pile of magazines from the only armchair in the room, stack them on the floor, and sit down. All in slow motion. All to give myself time to think. Finally I say, "Céline owes me one."

"One what?" she growls.

"What do you think kept me going in academia?" I growl back. "The women's studies seminars?"

Simone whips off her smudged-denim painter's apron and slings it across the room. Then steps in front of me, chest heaving under her white Beatles T-shirt. Their four smiling faces, drawn in red, are now bobbing on and about her braless breasts. Bare feet planted about a yard apart, Simone jams her fists into her jeans pockets, arms akimbo, eyes targeting mine and unmoving. It's the kind of hold-your-ground stance that forest rangers tell you to take should you come upon a mountain lion in the wilderness.

From my poker days with little Dickie Halloway, I learned not to tip my hand until the eleventh hour. But the eleventh hour is striking now, and I'm going to have to lay a few cards on the table.

"We have to go back to my early days in Santa Barbara," I begin. "At the University of California. After Céline became the department chair and my one buddy-in-residence."

"Buddy? How quaint!"

I bypass Simone's verbal smirk and go on: "We had the most arrogant Dean you can imagine. We both hated his guts. So when he put Céline in charge of directing a conference, complete with book and art exhibit on Apollinaire, I got the brilliant idea of forging a letter."

"Who's Apollinaire?"

"Turn of the century French poet," I say, omitting a comment on Simone's abominable ignorance. "The letter was to his mistress, Marie Laurencin. I had his handwriting scanned by a graphics outfit in San Diego who had never heard of Apollinaire either, and with them and my computer the first letter came out beautifully. And in cyberspace, I placed a reference in an old document -- "

"First letter?"

"Followed by a second and a third. From a 'Private Collection' in France. The Dean was gaga. Céline told him that the lender wished to remain anonymous, but that she finally got the Countess in question to reveal herself. And come to Santa Barbara -- all expenses paid, of course -- to be the focal point of the conference." I pause. "So? No applause?"

"Fatal flaw number two: you think you're above the

law."

"There are only two kinds of people, Simone. Those who are slaves to the law and those who interpret it for themselves."

"Yes, master."

"Anyway, Céline's Countess -- whom you now know -- was a real countess all right, an old friend and Guérillère, and she loved my Apollinaire affair. She also seduced Céline away from academia, and that's when she moved back to Paris. We sold my letters here -- on the black market, needless to say. After that, you came along, and I lost touch with Céline."

"You could go to jail for selling those letters. For taking advantage of someone's trust."

"If that someone believed they were authentic letters, what's the difference?"

"I know, I know. Dog food in the meat pie again."

"It's like giving someone a gift." I pause to let that sink in. "Anyway, this evening I steered the conversation in the direction of my Apollinaire letters and then on to his involvement in the missing statuettes from the Louvre. To ease Céline and the Countess into our caper."

Simone lifts her hands, palms up, to indicate total ignorance of my reference.

"Apollinaire's secretary, a guy named Pieret, stole the statuettes for a lark, and shared them with Apollinaire and Picasso."

"You're making this up."

"Check it out. Do a little research for a change. You'll find that the statuettes were stolen in 1907, to be exact."

Simone shrugs. "So?"

"So a few years later, Pieret went off on another lark. That's when he stole a stone head from the Louvre."

"You're serious?"

"Check it out, Simone," I snap. "Check it all out. How somebody stole the Mona Lisa, too, and how that gave

51

Pieret the idea to contact a newspaper and tell them he had been informed about the stone head and that the thief would return it for a price."

"So he returned it himself and pocketed the money?"

My crooked grin says yes. "To make a long story short, Apollinaire got implicated in the affair. Falsely, I might add. And he spent a week in jail. And that's where he wrote my famous letters."

"Letters from the slammer," states Simone prophetically.

"You may also be interested to know that the thief who did steal the Mona Lisa had several copies of her made before the heist."

Simone squints at me. "Copies?"

"And right after the theft he sold them like hotcakes on the black market."

"And each buyer thought he was getting the real one?"

"My little naive pumpkin, the world is full of fake masterpieces." I give Simone another crooked grin. "So you see, my plan for the Marmottan is in the Grand Tradition. And Céline and the Countess loved it. They think Les Guérillères will, too." I fold my arms and tilt my head back. "Now, you decide. Once and for all. Are you with me?"

"You told them everything?"

"Of course not. Certainly not about our replacement Monet."

"You haven't even told ME how we're replacing it."

I bypass the implication and proceed with my agenda. "I told them only the basics. That we would steal a painting and then return it the same day, together with a scathing statement shaming the museum's security system and -- more importantly -- building notoriety for the Guérillères."

"I don't get it."

Too bad. "I also found out that Céline has it in for one of the curators at the Marmottan," I go on. "Just our luck, huh? Also that she and Countess Claire are spending next week-end with the head Guérillère, Margo Duc. In her country estate near Chartres. Céline offered to get us invited, too!"

"We'll see. *Sunrise* -- "

"*Sunrise* will wait."

"I'm having problems."

"The problems will wait too. Margo Duc won't."

"Look." Simone slouches over to her easel. "This industrial muck of Le Havre. Monet must have laid that in blue-grays over the dull sunset colors, then added all the other reflections in the front. Looks like he cleaned his brush out around the edges of the painting. In fact, the edges make it look like it was painted while still in a frame. Which is really odd. I mean like who's going to carry a frame to a paint site?"

I shrug, unable to come up with a rejoinder for that one.

"G.B., I don't know if I can do this."

"Yes, you can."

"Can I?"

"You can do anything you set your mind to." I seize the moment. "And this is what's going to help you!" I exclaim, waving in her face the pages of my manuscript that just minutes ago I retrieved from the floor by the front door.

"You think?"

"I know so. You just need to work it through. All part of the healing process."

"Healing process," she murmurs.

"Read this with me?"

"I don't need to read it."

"Then let's role play?"

"Maybe."

Her mellowing tone inspires my Mr. Bennett baritone: "Before we broke for lunch, Mrs. Gretch," I recite, fairly accurately, "we were talking about when you left Simone's Palm Springs residence on November 18, 1983.

Would you tell me the circumstances that led to your leaving?"

My gamble works. Simone gives me a raspy and almost verbatim Aggie: "We had discussed the fact that she -- uh -- she was going to have a -- uh -- well, that professor was coming down from Santa Barbara and because of that I could possibly make other living arrangements so that she and, well, so that, well, her house would be free."

"Simone asked you to leave, is that correct?"

"Not exactly. She asked me to make arrangements or suggested to make arrangements not to be at the house that Thanksgiving week-end when Eva was coming down." Here Simone snorts and shifts gears. "I can't believe your name is Eva, G.B. Who would ever call you Eva?" she giggles.

"My mother," I tell her solemnly. "Now Mrs. Gretch," I go on, even more solemnly, "prior to November of 1983, had Simone asked you to move out?"

"Not actually to leave the house in a permanent sense, that I knew of. We had sat and talked about Simone's arrangement with Eva Hopfinger and her flying back and forth to Santa Barbara and, you know, the fact that they were going to enter into whatever they were going to enter into there, and this arrangement of whatever they were, which I am not aware of, and as I find out, I was very unaware of."

It is my turn to giggle. "You sound more like Aggie than Aggie!"

"I had enough practice."

Then I fake Mr. Bennett's impatient, "You must realize that you haven't answered my question, Mrs. Gretch."

"Mr. Bennett, Simone and I were the same friends and had the same relationship that we had always had, and there was, you know, in my mind, no dissension whatsoever between us."

"So this discussion about your leaving took place when?"

"Not my leaving, but of her living her life and so

forth, and I had said I don't know how many times, now baby, when Eva's going to be down here, I'll go on up to Yucca Valley to cousin Bertie's place on week-ends or what have you."

"Isn't it true that on several occasions during the summer of 1983 Simone offered to help you find your own apartment? And you refused? And did she not finally give you an ultimatum to move out of the Palisades Drive premises totally and completely by Thanksgiving Day?"

"When she told me to get out?"

"Yes."

"Uh-huh."

"Where did you go?"

"I went into one of the burned-out buildings on one of the properties because we were going to have a big garage sale."

"How long were you intending to stay in the burned-out building?"

"Well, Simone had started running back and forth to Santa Barbara, and I hadn't had the garage sale."

"Well, all of that is non-responsive. How long was it your intention to stay in that burned-out building? Would you answer that, please?"

"Through the garage sale. Probably thirty days or something, two weeks, I don't know, whatever it took."

"And what did you take with you when you moved there?"

"The clothes I had on, and three dogs."

"Now Mrs. Gretch -- "

Simone puts her hands to her face and begins rocking back and forth. "No more, G.B." Her voice has cracked, and I could swear she has tears in her now hidden eyes.

"Baby, what's wrong?"

"Don't call me Baby, Aggie."

"Pumpkin?"

Simone looks up at me, a sphinx now and inscrutable.

"Why are you doing this, G.B.?" she asks dryly.

"I've told you why. It's a novel about the healing -- "

"No." Now her eyes are like searchlights, shooting off in different directions. "Maybe you should call it *The Boomerang*."

"*Boomerang?* I want a title with multiple meanings."

"For sure."

"Look, it's late." I take Simone's arm and direct her towards the bedroom. "You know my greatest concern is your well-being. You're the most important person in this world to me. My Priority Number One. My passion. Let me show you...yes?"

I give her a kiss on the neck that nets me a smile. It is more than a yes smile. It smacks of sweet surrender.

As we thrash about in the biggest bed in all Paris, Simone is all arms and legs, not her usual modus operandi. But hey, I'm all for surprises. I begin to chant, "I love you! I love you! I love you!" It drives Simone totally crazy, and I will spend the entire next day recuperating from her assorted amorous aerobics.

CHAPTER EIGHT

"Whap, bonk, whap, bonk!"

I step inside the apartment. Simone's ghetto-blaster is rattling the windows. Sounds like Shostakovitch to me. I prop my packages on the bar and head for the source.

"Hi. I'm back."

Simone is standing in front of her easel, staring at her *Sunrise*, and barely acknowledges my hello kiss.

I ask, "How can you paint with this noise pollution?"

"Can't you do two things at the same time, G.B.?"

"You don't sound very happy."

"You got that right. Between that old dyke and her three dogs and this Monet I'm goin' screamers!"

Whoa! A good thing I stopped at the market. "I have just what you need," I whisper seductively. "Picked up a bottle of Saint Emilion and a ring of boudin." Then I spot her waste basket. "What's this Mumm bottle doing in the trash?"

"Can't you see? It's empty. Empties go in the trash."

There is Nemesis Night in her tone. Good thing I stopped at the bookstore, too. Simone could buy herself anything she wants, but she's a sucker for gifts. As any anthropologist knows, gifts create a sense of indebtedness in the receiver.

"I also wandered by Shakespeare & Company," I say, "and got you an English translation of *Les Guérillères*, so you won't have to struggle with it in French."

"Rub it in!" is what I get from her instead of a thank you. "Just what I need. More to read. Bet you'll get me a

57

fuckin' library card next."

"My, we are in a bad mood, aren't we?"

"We? No. Me. Me."

"Okay, let's start over. Did you go back to the Marmottan?" I ask, assuming that much against my wishes she did.

"You know I did."

"Gave the Monet another appraisal?" Silence. Time for a major diversion. "Well, I had a great time in the Luxembourg Gardens," I tell her pleasantly. "Checked out the rear of the Senate building and the area near the guardhouse, complete with mustached guard in blue uniform and pillbox hat. There's a bench -- not too close, not too far away -- that's a perfect spot for...but that's my little secret."

"Blah, blah, blah," says Simone.

"Anyway, the guard had to yell at me for walking on the grass. The pigeons can do anything on it they please -- eat, excrete, copulate -- but no human toe must touch it."

I pause for a nod of agreement about Parisians and their precious little patches of public grass but get another "Blah blah" from Simone. "So I sat down on a bench for awhile," I go on. "The little elementary school kiddies were going home carrying knapsacks filled with books that weigh about as much as they do."

Simone's reaction is a sarcastic, "How touching!"

Maybe I can snare her with something lyrical. "Wish you had seen the clouds, dancing over the branches of the chestnut trees -- "

"So who has time to watch the clouds?"

I soldier on. "Then two young American women sat down near me and one asked the other, 'How do you say I really don't know in French? *Je ne vraiment sais pas?* Or *Je vraiment ne sais pas.*' Neither one right. I had to chuckle to myself -- "

"Hilarious."

"And then they started exchanging nocturnal secrets

in English, sure that no one could understand. So provincial!"

"Right, G.B. I've heard your old one-upmanship stories before, remember? People are so ignorant, as in *ignore* -- not to know."

I could run with that one, but I decide on a new direction: "Two things you see in the Luxembourg these days -- joggers and cans of Coke Lite. Times change."

"The worm turns, as Aggie would say."

"So I sat there on the bench, thinking about our lark."

"There will be no lark."

"Pardon?"

"No lark."

"Okay, Simone. I understand. You're nervous because you don't know my plan. You -- "

She is all sarcasm with, "You have a plan?"

I am unruffled. "It's best I keep the details to myself."

"Not anymore. No more secrets, no more cliffhangers, G.B. An idiot can figure out that we can't tiptoe into the Marmottan and switch my *Sunrise* with Monet's -- even with your Guerilla Girls hovering about. There are employees around called guards. How do you say guard in Latin?"

I nod towards the armchair. "Let's sit down?"

"Not unless you're going to tell me everything. Do you hear me? EVERYTHING!"

There is high noon and gunsmoke in her tone. I bow slightly to signal agreement and take her hand. This time she lets me lead her to the chair, and she sits down on my lap.

"Was garlic guard in the Marmottan today?" I ask.

Simone grimaces. "Close enough to turn my stomach."

"Perhaps you noticed that he is unarmed?"

She searches the wall for a vision. She finally mutters, "Umhum."

I continue: "All nine of them are."

"Of them?"

"The museum's nine guards."

"Maybe they have hidden Magnums."

"Nonsense. We'll have fake guns, by the way. No ammunition."

"A regular Peace Corps operation, huh?" she sneers.

"One of our cohorts, of course, will be our driver. The others will take the two upstairs floors. Lock the guards and visitors into the room of miniatures. Meanwhile, we'll flush out all the people downstairs. March them upstairs for safe keeping. Then you and I'll go back down and put two Monets in our portfolio."

"What portfolio?"

"The large and sturdy portfolio we take in with us. Our companions will think that we're bringing it in to collect a Monet. But it will not be empty."

"No, of course not. It'll have a machine gun to be assembled in the john -- "

"Your fake."

"My fake?"

"So we go out with two Monets."

"One of which will be *Sunrise*?"

"And the other Monet's *Sunset*. Two paintings but only one empty space on the wall downstairs."

Simone's lips have parted now in awe and excitement. "Ooooo" is all she can say.

"We zoom out onto the Boulevard Périphérique and disappear in traffic in minutes."

"Ooooo."

"We pick up our own car -- "

"We have a car?"

"We will have. And we'll also have a note of explanation for the police."

"Signed, 'Love, Gang Bang.'"

"'Love, Les Guérillères.'"

Simone is squinting at me again. "Why would your so-called underground intellectuals go for that?"

"You're getting ahead of my story. What matters is that they will know nothing about the Simone Franklin original hanging in the Marmottan. What's more, the Police won't even care about catching up with us."

"Of course not. They'll appreciate my original."

"They won't ever know. We're going to leave the portfolio with *Sunset*, together with the note, of course, on a bench -- "

"Aha! In the Luxembourg Gardens?"

"Yes, my sweet Pumpkin." I give Simone a kiss on the forehead for at last putting two and two together. "And *Sunset* gets returned immediately to the Préfecture de Police. Why, it may even be back in the Marmottan by Sunday afternoon!"

I take advantage of the moment and slip an arm around Simone's shoulders. She tilts her head back and closes her eyes. I find myself playing with her hair, nuzzling her neck, murmuring yumyum sorts of things, expecting at any moment to receive my just desserts. But I can feel her body begin to stiffen. Then she pulls away and her eyes snap open.

"No!" she says defiantly.

"What now? What's come over you, Simone?"

"*Sunrise*. It's a bitch! Monet did it wet into wet, but I've got to let mine dry. Well, he let it tack up overnight maybe or a couple of days, but I have to let it dry, because I have to reproduce every friggin' brushstroke. Even Monet couldn't recapture his own spontaneity, so how am I supposed to?"

"Hey, take it easy. You're beginning to act like you're drunk."

"Drunk as I can be and still be sober." Simone pushes up off my lap and slouches over to her easel. "I can't paint *Sunrise*," she whines, and grabs a palette knife.

Knowing her destructive tendencies, I envision ugly slashes in her canvas. It is time for me to walk on water. "How about unclenching that knife?" Gingerly, I move across the room. "Number one: you can do it. Number two: we're going to meet the infamous Guérillères this week-end. And...number three...hey, there's nothing to cry about."

I wrap both arms around her and Simone snuggles wet eyes into my shoulder.

Her "I'm not crying" comes out garbled.

"Come on now. Control yourself."

That jerks her to attention. "Now that's really what I need to hear," she squawks. "Controlled spontaneity, oh, sure. I feel like one of those Andalusian horses we saw in Vienna. They've got all this power, like they could just fly to the moon, but they've got to do these tight little jumps and kicks. Control, shit! I've got to be free. Monet was free. *Sunrise* is really a loose oil sketch, you know. How do you think I can match his every brushstroke that was done freely? Impromptu?"

"You will." I attempt to cradle her in my arms. "Pumpkin, you're just going through one of those stages, like the writer before the blank page. You need a little distraction, that's all. Like this blast of a week-end."

"Hngghh!"

"Just think, Margo Duc, the Guérillères' ring leader. Fabulous, fabulous lady. As one of my former profs at the Sorbonne once said, *Elle a couché avec tout Paris*, meaning -- "

"Yeah, yeah, so she's slept with all Paris."

"She's been around -- "

"Forever."

"Since the days -- "

"Days of Yore, when the quays were two-way streets."

"With horses and buggies."

"Whores and buggers."

"My, my. Aren't we foul-mouthed this evening. You, I mean." I really can't stand Simone's vulgar streak, but in the interest of peace I resist the temptation to tell her about it and proceed instead with: "Anyway, Margo Duc has traveled absolutely everywhere."

"And done everything."

"That's what they say."

"I have done nothing and never will."

Simone's swings into total lack of self-esteem never fail to melt me. I patiently continue: "You know, Margo has rubbed shoulders with most of the greats of our century."

"More than shoulders, it sounds like."

"Take André Breton. An *ami intime*, according to Céline. That whole surrealist troupe of painters and poets -- Eluard, Aragon. And Margo was the model for the heroine of at least one novel."

"Blah, blah, blah."

"Also, Céline said Margaret Jefferson Hunt is still alive."

"From Aggie to Maggie."

"Now Maggie was once a real beauty, I'll tell you. This from old photos I once saw at Céline's. And what a class act Maggie is! She comes from the best of families. Eastern seaboard. All Harvard and Yale and tons of money. Unfortunately, she developed a problem with booze."

"Booze, booze, booze."

"But when she's on the wagon, Maggie's all boom and brilliant conversation. Anyway, through her and Céline it'll be a cinch to get three or four people to do the heist with us."

"There will be no heist."

"No heist?"

"No heist. No hoax, no heist."

I can lose patience too. I snap, "What do you mean?"

"What do I mean?"

"Yes?"

"I mean, I can't paint it. Do you hear me? I can't paint *Sunrise*. I'm a failure. I'm the fake. I can't do it. Can't! CANT!"

This is followed by a spine-tingling outburst that contains some of the most godawful sounds I have ever heard in my entire life, from snarls to dry gargles. In desperation I do my imitation of Marcel Marceau riding the

Katherine E. Kreuter

métro, usually a shoo-in to cheer her up, but no go.

Simone now grabs two silver candlesticks from her Renaissance credence -- all of which she spent a fortune on recently at an antique auction at Fantoches -- and bops herself on the head with them. Right hemisphere, whap! Left hemisphere, bonk! Whap, bonk, whap, bonk, until I finally wrestle her to the floor and hold her fast, amidst the shards of a broken Baccarat flute and assorted overturned potted plants. All of the above, by the way, to the accompaniment of Shostakovitch's Seventh Symphony blaring its brass on her stereo all the way from Paris to Perestroika.

Finally, the storm passes. I get my Claudia Monet to take a steamy soothing bath. ("They give schizos hot baths." So saith Simone.) A cozy spring fire in the bedroom fireplace follows, together with a cup of hot chocolate, a hot water bottle, and lots of pillows to snuggle among in the biggest bed in all Paris. And Simone is soon fast asleep.

Unable to doze off myself after all the fireworks, I finally give up and go into my study and put the finishing touches on the next chapter of my *Deposition*.

I breeze through the last few pages, where Mr. Bennett grills Aggie on the doctors she has been seeing: Dr. Heinemann about her dizziness, perhaps attributable to hypoglycemia; Dr. Perron for laryngitis; Dr. Stoltz for a severe eye problem that Aggie calls "going blind." With a smile, I proofread the next section:

BY MR. BENNETT:
Q. What other doctors did you see?
A. Dr. Madson.
Q. Do you mean the veterinarian in Rancho Mirage?
A. Right. The three dogs had all come down with ear infections and --
Q. I am not inquiring about the dogs, Mrs. Gretch.

I burst out laughing. "Oh, Aggie," I say aloud, "Even

I can't believe you're real." Then I scan the next part, when Bennett finally gets out of Aggie that she went to see a Dr. Feigenbaum:

Q. Why did you see Dr. Feigenbaum?
A. I was sent to Dr. Feigenbaum by the county because of Simone's...what would I call those...when she had...I can only think of the word accusations...when she had me arrested...and harrassed...and -"
Q. What kind of a doctor is Dr. Feigenbaum?
A. What kind?
Q. Yes?
A. A shrink.
Q. I see. Why don't we continue on another day? The Court Reporter will be relieved of her duties in regard to that transcript under the code. The deposition will be signed under penalty of perjury.

BY MR. CARNEY: So stipulated.
(THE DEPOSITION WAS ADJOURNED AT 4:30 P.M.)
(STATE OF CALIFORNIA)
(COUNTY OF RIVERSIDE)

CERTIFICATE
OF
DEPOSITION NOTARY PUBLIC

I, DOROTHY HOWELL, CERTIFIED SHORTHAND REPORTER AND NOTARY PUBLIC OF THE STATE OF CALIFORNIA DO HEREBY CERTIFY:
THAT THE FOREGOING DEPOSITION IS THE ORIGINAL DEPOSITION TAKEN BEFORE ME AT THE TIME AND PLACE THEREIN SET FORTH, AT WHICH TIME THE WITNESS WAS DULY SWORN BY ME;
THAT THE TESTIMONY OF THE WITNESS AND ALL OBJECTIONS MADE AT THE TIME OF THE EXAMINATION WERE RECORDED STENOGRAPHICALLY BY ME AND WAS

*THEREAFTER TRANSCRIBED, SAID TRANSCRIPT
BEING A TRUE COPY OF MY SHORTHAND NOTES
THEREOF AND A TRUE RECORD OF THE
TESTIMONY GIVEN BY THE WITNESS.*

*IN WITNESS WHEREOF, I HAVE SUSBSCRIBED
MY NAME AND AFFIXED MY SEAL THIS DATE:*

FEB 28, 1986

_____.

Dorothy Howell

_____

Notary Public - California
Riverside County
DOROTHY HOWELL, C.S.R.
 My commission expires:
 October 4, 1986
 CERTIFICATE NO. 3742

I sign the document myself, giving Dorothy Howell's signature an elementary school teacher's careful script to match the riotously methodical Ms. Howell I observed when Aggie was being deposed. Then I put these last pages of Part I of my novel in a folder which I'll give to a bruised and sheepish Simone to read in the morning. But not until after she has had three cups of cappuccino and two huge buttery croissants that I'll purchase shortly after dawn at the boulangerie around the corner.

On second thought, maybe tomorrow I'll just keep the chapter to myself. Give Simone a day off. And give myself a breather. Not my usual style, but hey, whatever works. The trouble is, something is bothering me, and I can't figure out what. Or who. And what did Simone mean by *The Boomerang?*

I prop my feet up on my desk, tilt my chair back, fold my hands behind my neck, and give my Pumpkin's psyche some further attention. Somehow I need to get her to distance herself from the past. Make some sort of closure. Live for today. But how?

Maybe it's better to save Margo Duc and a week-end in the country for later. Yes. And schedule some diversionary entertainment for tomorrow. Yes, that's it. Something really different for just the two of us. Do a few cartwheels around Paris. After all, tomorrow is Sunday. And we both deserve a day of rest.

CHAPTER NINE

"The larger the candle, the bigger the sin."

Yesterday was one of those incredibly balmy Sundays in May with a sky so blue -- cobalt blue, according to Simone -- that we knew it would never, ever rain again. From our living room window, we could see the hill of Montmartre in the distance. Capping it, the white domes of the Church of the Sacré Coeur glistened in the sunlight. Yes, we would go there. And yes, we would make our pilgrimage on foot.

We took our time crossing the Pont Neuf, watching the barges in the Seine slip slowly under the footbridge beneath our feet. Then, on the Right Bank, we skirted the Louvre and stopped for coffee in a sidewalk café on the Avenue de l'Opéra. From there we followed the Rue Pigalle up to the Place of the same name, dubbed Pig Alley by post-war G.I. Joes.

Both the street and the square were speckled with pimps who seemed to favor checked suits. The prostitutes -- even in their Sunday best -- looked to us like the answer to no lord's prayer. Simone, of course, had to diss each one, plus every stripper in every photo in the window cases of the red-light night clubs.

Whores leaned out of shady doorways all the way up the Rue des Martyrs, their eyes tied with scarlet-ribboned invitations to paradise. In broad daylight they were garish. One displayed her wrinkly wares through a nearly transparent dress which fell indecently below her dimpled knees. She nevertheless attracted the urgent attention of two wiry young

Senegalese, who came whirring towards her like arrows to a bullseye.

Another tired *putain* ambled behind us for a block or so, her flaxen hair tied with a rubber band into a knot atop her head. One gnarled hand clutched a string bag of groceries; the other fiddled with a cigarette. Even from twenty paces, her rusty perfume scratched our nostrils.

It was nearly noon when we climbed the final flight of steps up to the Sacré Coeur. There, all Paris lay at our feet. The air was so clear we could reach our magic fingers far across it and touch the copper-green spires of Notre Dame and the distant dark nippled dome of the Pantheon. We were breathless with beauty.

Arm in arm we went inside the church, into a flickering dimness exquisite with incense. Simone led me directly to a rack of candles and examined several candidates before she chose a slender white taper. (Only Simone can tell white church candles apart.) She insisted on this four franc variety rather than the larger eight and twelve franc specimens.

"Less conspicuous," she whispered to me. "The larger the candle, the bigger the sin."

We lighted it ceremoniously and together placed it before a statue of Sainte Thérèse, who seemed contented to go on hugging her stone crucifix and reified roses for all eternity.

Feeling touched by all the deities that had ever announced themselves from Buddh-Gaya to Galilee, we floated half a block away into an Italian hole-in-the-wall restaurant. Its inner garden beckoned with a half-dozen Cinzano-umbrellaed tables and Van Gogh bedroom-in-Arles chairs. And a Neapolitan piano player so bad that we were enchanted all the way through three pizzas dark with anchovies -- Simone adores them -- and two chilly bottles of Rosé d'Anjou.

Sainted, saturated and stuffed, we finally reemerged

into the maze of narrow streets that program movement on Montmartre. It wasn't long before we stumbled upon the junk shop where, one rainy afternoon in April, we had bought an old canvas Simone said was just what Claude Monet must have painted *Sunrise* on. And which, if all goes as planned, will soon be attracting attention in the Marmottan.

Today we poked around its shelves of dusty paintbrushes, tired puppets, demented old dolls, and squads of lead soldiers in Napoleonic gear that looked as if they had indeed fought half a dozen campaigns. Then suddenly Simone spied a tube of Parisian green paint.

"It has arsenic in it!" she let me, the owner, and the other two customers know. "It's illegal!"

But, of course, the Impressionists used it, and so would she. I purchased it for her, along with a tube of lead white, also extremely toxic, according to Simone. But Monet used it, and so would she.

"Besides, lead white doesn't yellow," was her last canon of the day.

We drifted on into the Place du Tertre. As usual, the square was teeming with con artists threading the crowds, and would-be artists doing portraits of mostly camera-strung tourists. My guess was that these had been let out of their buses, following a somber BEWARE lecture from their guide, and were momentarily expecting to find somebody else's fingers in their pockets.

On one corner were four young Peruvian musicians working magic with their flutes and guitars. Even the poor and the elderly tossed coins into their collection hat -- gold and silver thank-yous for transforming their winter into springtime for those few precious moments.

On another corner huddled a semi-retired bum selling a giant fistful of balloons waving red and yellow and green against our cobalt-blue sky. Giddy Simone picked out a red one for her third gift of the afternoon and carried it off in a tight little fist.

We, too, drifted upwards with the red balloon, glowing in our own candled sunlight, afloat somewhere over the cobblestones and trickling gutters of Montmartre on waves of sound and color, on air as light and cushiony as an eiderdown. We had merged with that blissful blur of humanity, diffused into a single flowing tapestry. We/They had become one seamless fabric upon which our ordinarily obscured feelings for our fellow unknowns began to pop out of an inner darkness like streetlamps at dusk. Floating islands of timelessness in an undifferentiated space. Shapeless. Eternal. For that whole long lovely Sunday afternoon in May.

CHAPTER TEN

"I had a habit of eating myself."

    This morning it is raining again, I am writing again, and Simone is again painting. Now armed with arsenic green, she is determined today to finish with "the vermilion glob of paint" left on her palette. And I am just as determined to do justice to Aggie in my next chapter.

    I take her original deposition out of a desk drawer and look over the beginning of Volume II. Since I'll be changing the names later, I see no reason not to print out the opening paragraph just as it is:

    THE DEPOSITION OF ELLA AGNES GRETCH, VOLUME II, TAKEN BEFORE SALLY S. SMOCK, CERTIFIED SHORTHAND REPORTER AND NOTARY PUBLIC IN AND FOR THE STATE OF CALIFORNIA, WITH PRINCIPAL OFFICES IN THE COUNTY OF RIVERSIDE, COMMENCING AT 10:15 A.M., MARCH 3, 1984, AT THE OFFICES OF BENNETT, BAINES & BOHRMAN, PALM SPRINGS, CALIFORNIA.

Then I proceed to the examination by Mr. Bennett:

    Q. Mrs. Gretch, you previously testified that when you left Simone Franklin's residence on the Saturday before Thanksgiving of last year that you were going to stay in a burned-out building on one of her properties.

    A. For the garage sale.

    Q. Where did you tell Simone you were going?

A. *I told her I was going.*

Q. *Going where?*

A. *Just going.*

Q. *Was this to be a permanent move?*

A. *Absolutely not. I was leaving for Eva to come down for Thanksgiving week-end.*

Q. *Did Simone ask you to return her keys?*

A. *Absolutely not.*

Q. *Did you not return her keys on the Wednesday before Thanksgiving?*

A. *She chased me into the street.*

Q. *For the keys? Keys? Keys?*

A. *Simone was going to call the police. That Eva was already dialing 911.*

I shake my head as I skim the next few pages of Aggie's deposition, reliving the street scene myself that Wednesday when Simone and I had driven down to Palm Springs from Santa Barbara for Thanksgiving vacation. As we pulled up in front of the Palisades house, there was Aggie, hustling a trio of pug dogs up into a pickup truck. Simone instantly came unglued.

"Aggie, my God, what are you doing here?" she screamed.

"Had to get some food fer the dogs," snarled Aggie. "They're yer dogs too, ya know."

It was the first time I had seen Aggie. I was shocked, in spite of everything Simone had told me. There stood Rosie-the-Riveter in a paint-splattered jumpsuit with work shoes to match. A cigarette was bobbing about in a corner of her mouth while her hands fussed with the dogs. They weren't responding well to her "Wanna go fer a ride, boys? Huh? Dontcha wanna go?"

Of course, Simone had given me the impression that Aggie had moved out. Apparently she did leave on the Saturday before, but when Simone left the house the next day, Sunday -- to fly up to Santa Barbara -- Aggie had already returned.

But no one can tell it like Aggie, a veritable Houdini at slipping out of ropey questions:

A. I had a doctor's appointment on Monday, so Sunday I had told Simone, Baby, I said, I don't have any clothes with me and I have to go to the doctor's tomorrow morning and so, you know, I'm going to stay here. And with that she got all upset and she said, my God, you can't stay here. I said what do you mean I can't stay here? What are you talking about? And she said, well, you just can't, Aggie. I said well, why can't I, and so we got into a sort of thing because here it was late in the evening and I was supposed to try to, you know, get some clothes and go to the doctor's in the morning. I had nothing down at the old burned-out building. Just a pad, a sort of bed, and the dogs' things --

Of course it's obvious that Aggie could have packed up some clothes on Sunday. And just as obvious, as I think about it now, that Simone could have insisted she do just that. Instead, Simone left and Aggie stayed. As she told Mr. Bennett, she stayed because she had never moved out.

Bennett then tried another detour, hoping to trick Aggie into a confession:

Q. Okay. Mrs. Gretch, was sex ever a part of your relationship with the defendant?
BY MR. CARNEY: That doesn't bear on any of the issues in this lawsuit. It's gone far enough, counsel. I instruct the witness not to answer.
BY MR. BENNETT:
Q. Mrs. Gretch, are you going to --
A. I'm not answering.

I sit back in my chair and stare into space. I wonder how Aggie would have answered that one had she been given a chance. For the first time, I let myself dwell on the details of the sexual relationship Bennett was trying to establish in order to net Aggie in an affair with a minor. Did she and Simone really have sex? I've never discussed that with Simone. Did I take it for granted? Maybe. Ignored it? Thought it preposterous? What on earth would it be like to have sex with Aggie? I imagine her pillow talk, something along the lines of: 'Was that as good fer you as it was fer me?'

While I am lost in my irreverent reverie, Simone appears in my doorway. I imagine Aggie coming up behind her, wrapping her Rosie Riveter arms about her waist. Simone's head sinks back on Aggie's shoulder....

Simone's "What evil are you up to now?" snaps me to attention.

My "Nothing!" smacks of guilt. I can't resist adding, "You know, you've never talked about your other lovers. Were there...many?"

"Like your string of firecrackers? No."

"But...others?"

"Aggie."

"Only Aggie?"

Simone nods in an odd, bemused sort of way, as the phone rings. When I answer it, Céline's crisp voice informs me that everything is arranged for the week-end, that she and the Countess will pick us up Friday morning at ten and drive us to Margo Duc's country estate. I thank her about six times before I replace the phone in its cradle and repeat the news to Simone. But she is staring at the manuscript on my desk and only half listens.

"You still think you're going to get that published?" she asks.

"I know so."

"I thought publishers like to sell books. Make money. That means fast plot and fun characters. So what's your secret?"

I feel semi-transparent. Once upon a time, Simone would never have dared to ask me that. "Somebody owes me one," I say carefully.

Her "Oh?" tells me that she intends to lean against the door frame and stare at me for all eternity or until I spill the story, whichever comes first.

"A guy named Bob Guethin," I begin. "I wrote a Master's Thesis for him that got him his degree at Yale and an office at Hutchins and Merrill. He's now a senior editor there."

Simone shakes her head. Then without a word wanders off.

I shrug and turn my attention back to Aggie's deposition. I decide to print out another page verbatim. Why try to render Aggie better than Aggie?

Q. Now, Mrs. Gretch, after you surrendered your keys and left the house that Wednesday before Thanksgiving, when did you next see Simone?

A. Well...it rained, yes, about a week later, and she came down to the old building to see if some furniture she had stored there was all right. That was when she came in.

Q. Did Simone know you were there?

A. She did when she saw me.

Q. You never told her where you were staying?

A. She assumed that I had taken an apartment, and where was it exactly is how she put it. Where's your apartment, Aggie? And I said, well, I'm not going to tell you right now, and she said, well, why not? I want to know where you're going to live. And I said, well, I'll let you know. Well, are you warm? Have you got the utilities on and everything?

Here again, her story is like Swiss cheese. First Aggie says she was leaving only for a matter of days. Who has utilities turned on for a matter of days? But again, Aggie wriggles out of it:

Q. Is it correct that you were to find an apartment just

for that long week-end?

A. No, not just for that week-end. As it turned out, you see, I was being deceived. She assumed --

Q. I don't want to know what she assumed.

A. I can only answer what I know.

And, of course, she knows nothing. I find myself wondering how many martinis Bennett must have put away when he finally finished with Aggie. But at that point he shifted gears again and pressed on:

Q. Okay, okay. Now Mrs. Gretch, between the Wednesday before Thanksgiving and the day Simone found you in the old building, about a week later, had you been back to the Palisades Drive residence?

A. No.

Q. You had not gone back there at all?

A. Had I seen Simone there you mean?

Q. No, that's not what I mean. Had you gone back to the residence?

A. Yes, I was back after Thanksgiving. On Sunday night.

Q. Did you know where Simone was?

A. I figured she had gone back up to Santa Barbara.

Aggie knew damned well that Simone had gone back up to Santa Barbara with me. What she didn't know was that before we left, I insisted we change the locks on the doors of the house. So when Aggie admitted to Bennett that she discovered the change when she tried to get in that Sunday night, he had a question for her that would sink most people: "How did you know the locks had been changed if you no longer had any of Simone's keys in your possession?" Aggie flicks that one off like a gnat off her sleeve: "I'd found a spare."

Undaunted, Bennett proceeds:

Q. Then what did you do?

77

> *A. I was a resident there. I changed the locks.*
> *Q. And entered the house?*
> *A. I was there, yes.*
> *Q. Did you remove anything from the house?*
> *A. I took money out of the Victorian chest.*
> *Q. Did you have a key to the chest?*
> *A. I knew where it was hidden.*

Now that I think of it, Simone knew that Aggie knew. Why didn't she switch the key to some other hiding place? It was like an open invitation to Aggie to go in. Needless to say, Bennett asked Aggie what she removed from the chest. Her answer:

> *A. I...at the time Simone had five hundred dollars in cash laying there in the chest and I took that. Borrowed it. I didn't have any money, Mr. Bennett, and Simone was in Santa Barbara, plus the fact that there's other reasons, but I don't think that Simone would be interested now, and I'm sure that you're not, but I had wanted to get the money because I was going to buy Simone a Christmas present.*
> *Q. I see.*
> *A. Plus the fact that I had three of her dogs who had to have some food, and it just so happened that I had a habit of eating myself.*

Eating herself! Oh, Aggie, what a verbal clown you are! And you don't even know it! You know something, Aggie? I thought of you yesterday. While Simone and I were standing in the glow of the great altar of the Sacré Coeur. While we listened to music on the Place du Tertre. While I watched Simone fly her red balloon. I thought of you...and I don't even know why. Maybe Simone is right, and I am obsessed by you and *The Deposition*. So what? *Les jeux sont faits.* And I'm not quitting now.

CHAPTER ELEVEN

"Buy the champagne; hold the poodle."

"Simone? You home?"

I've just closed the front door of the apartment and am calling into an eerie quiet. I hold my breath. No music. No sound. I can feel panic beginning to flap her wings in my chest. Could Simone have gone over the edge? She was merrily painting her *Sunrise* when I left, but that was a week-end ago.

The possibility that Simone could commit suicide has concerned me from Day One. She has no rudder, no anchor, no compass. And she obviously has a self-destructive streak that manifested itself in her recent whap/bonk episode which she blamed me for, of course. Said I was pushing her beyond her limits. But I know what she can and can't do, and I always manage her with care. I have made a reasonable mix for her of change and continuity, wildness and predictability. Simone doesn't know where one begins and the other ends. It's all one continuum to her: order-chaos-balance-confusion.

Here she is now, slinking out of our bedroom, wearing her dark Delilah eyes and the crimson satin negligée I gave her last Christmas. It's a deterrent to all rational thought.

Simone gives me a throaty, "I missed you."

"Playing in bed alone?" I surmise.

"Say what?"

"No music. You wanted to be able to hear the door."

"Screw you, G.B.!"

She plants a swift kick on my left kneecap, and I

buckle. I should know better than to make such an innuendo, but she caught me off guard. We have had umpteen prior scenes caused by my ability to see right through her. No, that's not quite right. Caused, rather, by her emotional upset over being transparent to me. According to Simone, her mother made her feel like an animated glass house, an image not lost on a variety of schizophrenics. Or their shrinks.

"Hey, just kidding!" I say, backing off.

Simone has caught my limp now and her eyes soften. I take advantage of the shift and say, "So ask me about the trip?"

"One of your absolutely brilliant intellectual gatherings, no doubt. So what happened?"

"Margo Duc asked about you. She began to think you don't exist."

"Me too."

"She would have adored you!"

"I wouldn't have fit in. Come on, G.B. Admit it. You really didn't want me to go. Thought I'd set the dogs barking again, like at La Mangerie. Think I'm not on to your plan? Divide and conquer, that's your strategy. You're just as transparent as I am."

"Let's get in bed and I'll tell you stories," I whisper in her ear. "Beddy-by stories."

I take Simone's arm and guide her into our bedroom. Nothing she likes better than to be told stories in bed. Mommie Dearest was obviously short on them, probably too tanked to talk by bedtime.

Simone props pillows against the enormous backboard of the biggest bed in all Paris, then props herself up against the pillows. Her long dark hair is aswirl around her face. Her negligée is brim-full with the most perfect breasts in the whole world. In shape and size, they inhabit that glorious zone halfway between Dolly Parton and Jodie Foster. These are breasts I'd like to set to music. Breasts with a bold rhythm. And shifting melodies. I stand there, like an utter idiot, listening to their siren's song.

"So tell me a story," begs five-year-old Simone.

I sense that the breasts will have to wait. I sit down on the edge of the bed. "Where do I start?"

"At the beginning? Through the middle and on to the end?"

"Such traditional narrative!"

"Better traditional than incomprehensible."

This remark reflects Simone's view of some avant-garde literature I tried to introduce her to, but gave up on.

"Well, once upon a time last Friday," I begin, "Céline and the Countess picked me up to begin our litle trip. Céline, by the way, asked me to drive. Because the Countess -- "

"The Countess couldn't drive a tricycle."

"Anyway, I am driving. And Céline is in the back seat with her notebook, which she writes in all the way to Rambouillet."

I imitate Céline, sprawled in the back seat of the car, and Simone giggles. Then I imitate myself at the wheel of Céline's Peugeot, watching her in the rearview mirror. More giggles from Simone. And then I imitate the Countess, working on her makeup, using the mirror on the visor. Simone guffaws.

"Well, we get to Orvilliers, hang a left at the village church, and turn off on a dirt road that skirts a thick stone wall, probably twelve feet high and all moss-covered. Then we follow the wall until we get to an enormous -- "

"Moat? Drawbridge? Dungeon?"

"Gate. With a heavy bell-chain, which we pull. The gate opens and there stands Margo Duc in a dazzling riding habit: black hunting cap and crop, white silk shirt with a Chinese red cravat, black jodhpurs and knee-high boots. With her snow-white hair, she was absolutely stunning!" I shake my head. "And you had to stay home -- "

"And paint your forgery."

"Our forgery."

Simone gives me another one of her sphinx stares. "Actually, it's my forgery."

I shrug. "And your choice of words. By the way, did you read my last chapter?"

"If I have to hear about those dogs one more time I'll never have a dog again."

"But I was going to buy you a little champagne poodle for Bastille Day."

"Buy the champagne; hold the poodle. So what happened at the castle?"

Here is where I kick my boots off and prop myself up on a couple of pillows next to Simone. "Well Margo, it turns out, is quite the horsewoman. You would have drooooooled over her stables. And talk about beds of tulips! Emerald green lawns, a guest cottage for the couple who take care of the place -- this marvelous stone mansion that dates from the Renaissance -- "

"Like half your friends, apparently."

"Margo just turned seventy and still rides every morning. Still entertains in -- "

"I know. The Grand Fashion."

"Céline isn't so old. Fiftyish. Neither is the Countess. Maybe in her sixties."

"Swinging."

I let my eyes, narrow now with irritation, tell Simone that she can knock it off or go without the rest of her story. She smiles and cuddles up against me, left breast snuggling my arm -- a temptation far more juicy than the old apple in Eden.

I take a deep breath. "You would have loved Margo's big French country kitchen, hung with copper pans of all possible shapes and sizes. Priceless antique dining table! And the living room! Walls hung with trophies of Margo's hunting trips to India. Elephant tusks, lion's heads, sofas draped with leopard skins."

"No human remains?" Simone blinks. "Sorry."

"So Margo shows me to my bedroom -- one of seven. An exquisite Napoleon III bed with yellow roses on the canopy that matched the bedspread and wallpaper. Leather armchair, huge desk with all sorts of writing materials in it, just waiting for inspiration to strike the lucky guest. I was in seventh heaven! Only you were missing."

"Your little lead soldier."

"And Margo's own upstairs study was incredible. Objets d'art from Tanzania to Timbuctoo. And to top everything off, she had a very special guest spending the month with her. Dinarova."

"Dina who?"

"Dinarova. The great Russian actress who came to France just before the war -- "

"Which war?" snickers Simone.

I ignore that one. "She was all the rage in Moscow in the 20's and 30's. And the toast of Paris in the 40's. We'll have to see some of her movies."

"Oh, whoopie!" smirks Simone. "Now I get silent films!"

"Why, she knew Eisenstein and -- "

"Rosenblatt."

"Cute, Simone. Very cute." I resist an urge to crush a pillow over her face. "Anyway," I go on, "there was Dinarova, in a burgundy velvet gown, draped over a medieval couch -- "

"Probably unable to get up."

"Still elegant. Still a beauty. But unfortunately -- "

"In a coma."

"Blind."

"Blind as she can be and still see?"

"Blind. Period."

"What then? Did Anastasia arrive?"

"Enough, Simone." I roll off the bed and get to my

feet. "Upset because you weren't there?"

"I'm not upset." Simone reaches out an arm and pulls me back into bed. "Come on, G.B.," she coos, "let's hear the story."

"Well, we all dressed for dinner, naturally. Margo was stunning in a black tux with bow tie."

"Don't I get a detailed description of her? Eyes? Ears? Hands? Legs?"

"Two of each. But you're going to meet her soon. And then you can describe her to me. Anyway, she went down to her wine cellar and came back up with -- guess what?"

"Sparkling water from the Fountain of Youth?"

"A champagne you couldn't buy in a store for a hundred bucks a bottle. This with a pâté de foie gras that just melted in the mouth. And then came -- "

"Shangri-la shrimp?"

"Goose eggs. And each one numbered. Goose egg number twenty-six, number thirty, number two -- "

"The deuce goose!" shrieks Simone.

I tell her quietly, "No."

"Well, what did the numbers mean?"

"The day they were laid. So you know which egg was most fresh, which one needed to be eaten first, like April 26th."

"Oh, great!" Simone pushes me away. "That's the big story? Numbered goose eggs? Didn't anything happen? No heart attacks? No strokes? Maybe a stumble and a broken hip? No? At least somebody's hearing aid went on the blink?"

"Macabre, Simone. What's the matter with you? *Sunrise* not going well again?"

"Guess I just had enough of the Old Folks scene before I met you." Simone gives me a penitent pause. "Can't you spare me the Aggiesque details? Just tell me about dinner?"

"Well, with roast beef we drank Châteauneuf-du-Pape

that -- "

"Got it: that couldn't be bought for a hundred bucks."

"Coq au vin Saturday, luncheon on the grass this noon of Coquilles Saint Jacques. All of the above with Dinarova's tales of stage and screen, Margo's of hunting in the Himalayas, Céline's sparkling quips, sublime images from the Countess -- "

"And your own profounds of mind that would have staggered Derrida himself."

"Thank you. And I had time to tell Margo all about our scheme."

"Your scheme."

"Which she absolutely -- "

"Adores."

"And she's going to help us. In fact, she's coming into Paris soon to see Dinarova off to New York, and you'll meet her."

"So why wasn't your Boston socialite invited to the bash?"

"Margaret Jefferson Hunt? Maggie's in California. Drying out in Rancho Mirage."

Simone processes that one in a flash and comes up with: "The Betty Ford Center."

"But she'll be back soon. End of story."

I smile down at Simone, who has slipped horizontal. Her hooded Delilah eyes are telling me I can have whatever I want.

"I missed you," she groans.

From the lacy edges of her negligée, two pink halfmoons are emerging.

"I missed you too."

"How much?"

Nothing to do but to show her how much.

CHAPTER TWELVE

"Send up a smoke signal or what?"

"How's *Sunrise* going?" This I ask cautiously, as always, from the living room threshold of Simone's studio. I never know what to expect from my Claudette Monet.

"Great!"

I saunter in, still testing the atmosphere, alert for any airborne surprise, from a flying paintbrush to a hurled expletive.

"I've got my palette mixed," says a cheeky Simone. "Finally got the system, to match colors, that's the secret of the Great Forgery, getting the right values to the color. See that? The sun looks vermilion. There's cerulean blue. See there? But I'm mixing gray with them to really get an on-target palette, a one and a two, three and a four value, easier than the Impressionists, who mixed complementary colors, like vermilion and cerulean blue to get a gray, but you can hit it quicker by estimating a patch of color -- "

Simone is rambling on again ad infinitum while she waves sticky brushes about, peers at her *Sunrise*, stands back, squints, rambles some more.

I stop her with: "I just had a phone call from Céline. You'll be happy to know that everything's set for tonight."

"My back hurts."

"It's Saturday. The Big Night! Les Guérillères!"

"You go. I paint."

"We go. You paint tomorrow."

"You pushy."

"They're all going to be there! Margo Duc plus

86

Margaret Jefferson Hunt!"

"You go."

"Nothing's going to be decided unless Margo and Maggie meet us both."

"Just when I'm really on a roll," complains Simone.

I give her a sympathetic, "Sorry about that."

I am also sorry that for this evening I will have to abandon my divide-and-conquer policy which I have had to enforce recently regarding Simone's stormy relationship with Les Guérillères. But all I need tonight is a few fruitful hours to lock in the four principles of my little drama and get Simone to briefly bond with them -- however superficially. Then she needn't see them again until the morning of the heist.

So I tell Simone pleasantly, "You must get to know the Countess this evening too. Madame Claire Navret is from the cream of French society, you know. *La crème de la crème!* She has been through everything. The War -- "

"Which one?" Simone bursts into laughter. "Ones?"

"Very funny. I trust you'll not display that sort of poor taste this evening."

"Leave me home and then you'll be sure."

When cornered, I learned long ago, stick to a strong narrative line. In my once-upon-a-time tone I say: "The Countess was captured by the N.K.V.D. in Lithuania in 1940 when she was there on a goodwill lecture tour."

"Yes, Mrs. Gretch, you've been over all that."

"Céline was just telling me on the phone how the Russians suspected Countess Claire Navret of subversive activities -- which, as it turned out, was true."

"She was probably fasting again. Definitely suspicious in Lithuania."

To move my plot along, I ignore her unkind remarks. "And then came endless interrogations, then imprisonment," I say. "First in Kaunas, then Siauliai."

"Famous places, I'm sure."

87

The geography lecture will have to come later. "Just act as if you've heard of them."

"You fake!"

"So now you have heard of them. Anyway, for her heroic behavior, the Countess was presented with France's highest honors -- "

"Hmmm. Look at that." Simone is squinting at her easel again. "As you get further away the chroma decreases."

"Farther away."

"Right. And the further away you get -- " Simone shuffles backward. "I've got to get out and buy more poppy seed oil. That's what the Impressionists used as a medium. Most people don't use it anymore because they don't want the paint to stay wet so long, but it also fluffs it up, plus, that way things don't yellow with age."

I clear my throat to signify my continued presence. "Hello?"

"I've got to fluff this up."

"Fluff it up later." I step behind Simone and untie her artist's smock and slowly slip it over her head, careful not to disturb the three-inch dangly pair of earrings -- gun-metal grey replicas of the Eiffel Tower -- that fly about her jaws on the slightest provocation. I toss the smock across the room, Simone style, turn her around and hold her at arm's length.

"The body I am addicted to," I tell her honestly, as my eyes leisurely survey the length of her, molded by a white cotton turtleneck shirt and black and white striped bib overalls.

I slip my arms around her and whisper, "You are my favorite work of art, you know."

"If you want your second favorite work finished, you'll leave me home alone tonight."

"If you stay home, you'll have to read."

"Uggghh!" Simone pushes me away. "The only person who could enjoy that so-called novel of yours would be another Aggie."

"If that's true, then it'll be a best seller. Think of all the Aggies there are in this world."

"There's no action, no sex, no character development, no plot, no beautiful prose, and no insight into anything. The way Aggie talks in circles makes me crawl the walls."

"But that's what makes her so fascinating. Circles aren't easy, you know. Most people soldier on through life in monotonous straight lines. One, two, one, two." Here I march about the middle of the room, turning square corners that would make a drill sergeant proud. Simone giggles. It's the perfect moment for me to add, "Aggie is a wonderful example of what we all find frustrating in our everyday lives: tautological thought."

"Tautology?" Simone's eyes search the ceiling for a missing page of Webster's.

I assume my podium stance and professor's tone: "Tautology is simply the repetition of some idea without making anything any clearer or adding any new information."

"No wonder I forgot it."

"But in the case of *The Deposition*, the reader finds space to add his or her own information, and thus crack the circles."

"Believe me, G.B., there is nothing for me to add to my reading."

"You haven't read my latest chapter -- the best one yet."

"It doesn't have much competition."

"Come into my studio? Read a few pages with me? They're really quite hilarious."

"What do I get if I do?"

I nuzzle her ear. "Anything you want."

Simone mellows and we go arm in arm into my studio, sit down together on the couch and read:

BY MR. BENNETT:

Q. Let's go back to that rainy day, Mrs. Gretch, when

Simone found you down at the old burned-out building the week after Thanksgiving. Did she tell you to get off the property?

A. No, she didn't. In fact, we talked about many many many things.

Q. And did she tell you to continue living down there?

A. She didn't tell me to continue. Didn't tell me not to, either. She was very friendly.

Q. In spite of the fact that you had had the locks changed on the doors and had taken money from the house?

A. Yes we did. We did have a very friendly day.

"Oh, sure, very friendly," mimics Simone. She jerks her head toward me, her Eiffel Towers banging about her mouth. "All I could think of that day was what's G.B. going to say when she finds out that Aggie's still around. Like, how the hell do I make her disappear. You had the pressure on me, Babe. Bigtime."

"You might have told me the truth," I say defensively.

"I didn't know what the truth was."

"Say again?"

"You gave me an either-or ultimatum, remember?"

"Well, what did you expect? That I would ask Aggie to move over in that double bed of yours so I could slide in? And Baby makes three?"

"Aggie and I were just friends then."

"Aggie had an emotional hold on you I couldn't believe!"

"She got me out of my mother's clutches."

"And right into her own!"

"Enough, G.B." Simone drops my manuscript in my lap and is in the act of getting to her feet when I grab an Eiffel Tower and say, "Oh, no you don't."

"Ouch!"

"Escaping a discussion in no way resolves the problem."

Simone plops back down beside me. "What's the

problem?"

"We both need to work through this deposition. Exorcize Aggie, once and for all." I gently pull Simone to me and put an arm around her. "Aggie was no fool, I'll say that for her." Simone's big brown eyes ask why and I answer: "She got you, didn't she? She got years of you."

Simone holds up the next page of my manuscript. "And she's still here."

"But not for long. Read on?"

Reluctantly, she does, and I along with her:

Q. Mrs. Gretch, you have stated that you saw Simone at about quarter to ten that same evening?

A. Right.

Q. What happened then, Mrs. Gretch?

A. I had been asleep about an hour and Simone knocked on the door. She came in and said to me, honey, guess what. And I said yes, what are you doing down here, it's so late. And she said I found you a place to live, honey, because this is no place in the world for you to be living, all of this junk and it's all burned out and all, so after I went home I looked in the papers and I found you a place to live, a cute little gingerbread house right up the street here and you'll love it. And I said what am I going to move up there for, and she said well, you don't have any stove here or nothing. You're just sort of camped out. And I said Baby, we've been through this all morning. I've got the old tennis courts for the dogs, you want me to keep the dogs down here and they want to be with me anyway, and so forth, and if I move up there...does it have a yard or what? And she said I don't know, it was pretty dark. I said, Simone, what are you talking about anyway? We went through this, Mr. Bennett, from about a quarter to ten until about two o'clock in the morning that Simone was insisting that I move into this gingerbread dump up the street, and I'm saying that I couldn't see any sense in it because of the fact that I was down here and the reason I was down here right now was to have this big garage sale.

I burst out laughing. "That's one of the best pages I've ever read! Anywhere! And you think readers won't enjoy this?"

Simone seems not to hear. "You wouldn't believe how she was living there, G.B. You would have taken pity on her, too. She had rigged herself up a hot plate. Had an old portable heater -- "

"And you were still paying the electric bill," I remind her.

"There was only one room that hadn't been totally burned in the fire. And part of a bath. Plus, the roof leaked."

"Just a few drops, according to Aggie." I pause, noting the guilt in Simone's eyes. Then add: "So you rented Aggie the gingerbread house, but she went back to your residence after we had changed the locks and changed the locks herself. And the next time you went home you had to change the locks again -- which you didn't tell me about, either, at the time."

"It wasn't important."

"Not important? That you were locked out of your own home? And had to change the locks a second time?"

Simone hangs her head. "What else was Aggie to do? She needed money. The dogs needed food."

"Yes, Mrs. Gretch, we've gone over all that. And you had a habit of eating yourself."

Aggie's line slices through the nascent argument, and we both have to smile.

I nuzzle Simone's left ear and blow on an Eiffel Tower. It does a little riverdance as I say, "And we have a habit of eating ourselves...."

Simone blows smoke rings at me with her tongue. "And I'm suddenly very hungry."

"Shall we finish the chapter and then indulge ourselves?"

"This is emotional abuse, G.B."

"Nonsense." I wave the last page at her. "It's Friday,

December second, remember? And Aggie moved into the gingerbread house? You had paid her first month's rent? Then Mr. Bennett asks her how long she lived there. Yes? Read her answer?"

A. One night. I got in there at five o'clock and I left the next morning.

Q. When did you tell Simone that you had moved back to the old burned-out building?

A. That Saturday morning I called her and told her.

Q. What did she say when you told her?

A. She said okay, honey, why? And I told her I had gone to bed in that gingerbread house and that somebody had tried to get in the front door and then had come around to the back and tried to get in, and I had put padlocks on the door to lock it up, and even then she wanted to know why I hadn't called the police, and I said at a quarter to two in the morning, without a phone, how in the hell could I get a hold of the police? Send up a smoke signal or what?

I burst out laughing again. "I love that line! A smoke signal!"

Simone ignores my enthusiasm. "End of chapter," she states. "Mealtime."

Before her lips can cover mine, I manage to say, "We should leave in about an hour, okay? The Guérillères will be waiting."

"Uhmm."

"Departure at ten."

"That's tautological."

"You do amaze me."

"So where are we going?"

"Going?"

"Yes, Mrs. Gretch, going?"

I can already feel the warmth of her mouth. All I can say is, "Just going."

CHAPTER THIRTEEN

"How could you do this to me?"

"How could you do this to me?" hisses Simone.

She unlocks the door to our apartment, steps inside, and slams the door in my face. Almost. I've braced for the action and catch the door with one foot. Then follow in her wake.

It is four o'clock in the morning that has followed the Big Night. We have walked home in silence but not in step. I trailed a pace or two behind, hoping that by putting some distance between us Simone would not offer Parisian late-nighters any audio-visual street entertainment. It worked. But now is when the in-fighting could get close. Time to walk on water again.

"Mature people sit down and negotiate," I say.

Simone strides into the bedroom. "You lived on college campuses too long," she calls out over one shoulder. "You have no memory of reality."

"Maybe I should never have left" slips out of me before I can censor it.

"Maybe you should go back."

I whip one hand in front of my face to snare the suit jacket Simone has removed and flung my way. "Maybe I will."

"You are such a fake."

"Okay, okay, let me run the evening by you once more," I say, matter-of-factly. "We had a lovely walk over to Place Saint Sulpice. And were late getting to our rendezvous because guess who had to feed the pigeons in the square?"

"Yada, yada," says Simone.

"And guess who had to listen to the church bells toll ten o'clock?"

"Yada, yada."

"Come on, Simone. Admit it. Wasn't it fun finding the entrance to what is probably the most fashionable lesbian bar in the world?"

"Oh, right, G.B. High adventure. Finding that non-descript door with a little slit in it, like some speakeasy in Days of Yore."

"The Kathmandu is known for its privacy. So?"

"The darkest bar I have ever been in. I was blind as I could be -- "

"And still see."

"And so smoky I could hardly open my eyes, so of course I stubbed my toe going up that little narrow circular staircase. And that bouncer almost didn't let us up there, either. Into the Great Inner Sanctum."

"Waitress, you mean?"

"Oh, pardon me. Waitress, right. In her man's shirt and pants. Loafers and white gym socks. Sherlock Holmes pipe."

"So? She was super friendly, once she knew who we were meeting. And it was great up there, with those low divans and tables. Walls of mirrors with twinkling lights behind them -- "

Simone snorts. "And there sat the most godawful quartet I have ever, ever seen in my entire thirty-one years."

"Well, Céline -- "

"The chihuahua in the same three-piece tweeds!" With that, Simone fires two high-heeled shoes my way, with deadly John Elway accuracy. I deflect them in a last-minute wave of my arms, pick the two Dolce & Gabbana missiles up from the floor and am very tempted to fire them back.

"And our dear colorless Countess Claire in another flimsy frock." Simone sails her skirt by me. "The N.K.V.D.

Katherine E. Kreuter

wanted that for questioning? Give me a break!"

"Simone, really." This I say as I snag her blouse in mid-flight.

Simone turns to face me, hands on hips, wearing only a bra and pantyhose now. A fly-me-to-the-moon kind of moment in spite of the cannon-smoke atmosphere. "Yes, yes, that 'ill becomes me.'" She mimics my alto voice, my academic speech. Then she shifts up to her creamy soprano and hits high C with: "How could you do this to me?"

I reach out to unsnap her bra, but she jerks away from me, unsnaps it herself, and whips it around overhead before she lassos the lamp on the dresser.

That does it. "I'm going to bed," I announce, and do just that. Fully clothed. On top of the bed. My side.

"And then the old greyhound has the gall to tell me that 'this evening's conversation should go no further than us.'" Off come the pantyhose now in three deft moves. "One thing's for sure," says Simone, waving the nylon aloft, "the chihuahua must have one hell of a time trying to screw her!"

"You have gone beyond simple vulgarity."

Simone is naked now and quivering with an exciting mix of anger and delight in her own retelling of the evening. "And then there's your Maggie Jefferson Hunt. Your socialite? That ratso dog? Bristles of hair sticking out of that faded stocking cap, north, south, east and west. In about as many colors. Bet she hadn't combed it for three weeks."

"That's not kind," I say, covertly enjoying her descriptions as well as her demonstrations. Bare breasts a-jiggle now, Simone prances back and forth in front of horizontal me, stretched out in the biggest bed in all Paris.

"And you call her shuffle a 'typical Radcliffe slouch'? Maggie's bent over from carrying home booze, not books."

"Be kind."

"And that ravaged face," Simone continues, knowing now that her performance is being tacitly appreciated. "Yes, I must admit, old Maggie still does have that hint of long-lost

96

beauty. Even with hairs hanging out of her nose."

"I liked her chin hair."

"That preceded her by at least an inch. And behind it that alcoholic jaundiced look. But, oh, the rig!"

"She obviously dresses in layers. Ready for any occasion."

"Any place. Park bench. Métro grates. You name it."

"You really do have a vicious tongue, Simone."

"And in what rag-bag did Maggie find that moth-eaten boa? And that skirt that sagged almost to her ankles? Topped by several layers of shirts, the outer one a flannel with patched elbows. Prints, stripes, plaids."

"Certainly not colorless."

"And the stockings!" howls Simone. "A gray gathering over those dilapidated tennis shoes. There she was, scuffling between tables -- "

"At least the tennis shoes matched."

"Hole for hole." Simone leans over me, hands on hips. "These are your underground warriors?"

"You gave Margo Duc more than one catchy smile."

"I have to admit I did like her. She looked really cool in that safari suit. Probably has her own tailor."

"Soft white hair -- "

"Black leather boots. And that jaunty red Robin Hood hat with a feather in it." Simone's posing now, her arms and hands forming the hat and feather. "Venetian silk cravat. And a real rakish twinkle in those golden eyes. A regular Maurice Chevalier. Ready for a chorus of 'Leetle Girls.'"

"She's no dog, right?"

"A cat maybe. A lion."

"A lioness?"

"I said a lion. I'd like to paint those golden eyes..."

"See why I didn't try to describe Margo to you?"

"Glance at her sideways and she'd have you in bed!"

"My, my, MY!"

"She makes stompin' Aggie look like milktoast! And this is your fabulous, fabulous lady?"

"Lady being generic."

"She thinks my name is Aggie. You had to call me Aggie."

"You had to do Aggie's 'Pardon me?' routine."

"Well, you -- and yours -- had to do your *ne plus ultra* Latin routines. In a geriatrics ward like our corner of the bar, it's a wonder you didn't dig up a few native speakers."

"I've had about all I can take."

"They should have all tried poppy seed oil."

"And not yellowed with age, yes, I got it." I lift my head from the pillow. "This is where I get ready for bed."

"No you don't, G.B." Simone's nostrils flare and she snags my arm as I attempt to get up. "First you answer me this: how could you do this to me?"

"Do what?"

"This. This! THEM!"

"Them?"

"You promised three slick burglars and a race car driver, not that senior-citizen quartet."

"It'll be a lark."

"Margo, Céline and the Countess in full drag with toy guns?"

"You'll see."

"And that rag lady from Radcliffe driving the getaway car? Oh, no, no, no." Simone holds her head in her hands and sways back and forth. "'I can't walk, but I can drive,' she says. A few belts to boot and we'll all wind up in the slammer. Really, G.B., HOW COULD YOU DO THIS TO ME?"

"You'll see what great disguises they'll come up with. They've all moved in top theater circles -- "

"Disguises?" Simone is squeezing both my arms now, and it hurts. "Just trade outfits you mean?" she screams. "Margo with the Countess? Ratso with Céline? Can't you just see Her Highness in the safari suit, Stone Butch in flimsy beige chiffon, Ratso in a three-piece tweed and the Twit wrapped in mothy boa?"

"Listen up, Simone. They're all we need. And if there should be a problem, they know -- "

"I know. Just everyone."

"You'll see. You'll come to appreciate them."

"You're crazy."

Simone's squeeze has turned into passionate aggression. I say, "Why don't we hang this conversation up and get into bed before sunrise."

"Sunrise...."

"And think of the nights we'll be going to bed under *Sunrise*." I glance at the ceiling. "And the days we'll go to the Marmottan to see a famous Simone Franklin original."

"Always dangling the carrot, aren't you, G.B.?"

"And you can't resist. Say it. Greedy Simone will not resist." We are standing now and I have her by the shoulders. "Repeat after me -- "

"I will not."

This she may say, but I can see that she's weakening. Her body is now pressed against mine, mound to mound, and I'm regretting not having shed my clothes earlier.

I give her my most seductive smile and a low, "Come on, say it. Greedy Simone -- "

"Why should I?"

"Because I'm going to make love to you," I whisper, sucking a special place on her neck that might just as well be her G-spot. Her hands clutch my shoulders and her legs lift and lock around my waist, and like the famous double-backed beast we rock about the room. "Come on, say it."

Simone flicks her tongue between my lips and whispers, "Greedy Simone will not resist."

CHAPTER FOURTEEN

"I could barf all over your lousy manuscript."

"Hey, come on. Get ready. I'm taking you to my Valhalla this afternoon." This I call out from the bedroom as I reach in the closet for a pair of white slacks. My position gives me a partial view of Simone, clad only in beige bra and panties, rigidly horizontal on the living room couch.

"I haven't finished the latest Adventures of Aggie."

"She'll keep. Come on, let's go."

"Mr. Bennett, I am unable to go."

I give her Bennett's baritone: "Okay, okay. It's like pulling teeth in here today." I pull on white slacks and a blue Sorbonne sweatshirt and search the floor of the closet for my white Nikes. "So, Mrs. Gretch, what's wrong now?"

"I'm sick."

"Laryngitis? Hypoglycemia? Deaf? Dumb?"

"All of the above. And much, much, much more."

I march out barefoot into the living room. "What's the matter? You look like paranoia personified."

"I could barf all over your lousy manuscript."

"Hey, give that to me -- "

"No."

"Now look, Simone. What have I done to deserve this?"

"You tell me, G.B. What have you done?"

"I've told it like it happened. You rented Aggie the gingerbread house -- "

"And she was back at the burned-out building the next day, driving me nuts. Or was it you driving me nuts,

G.B.?"

"Me? I wasn't there, remember? According to Aggie, you walked in on her and started beating on the wall and screaming, 'Aggie, my God, what are you doing here?' I believe she told our dear Mr. Bennett that you were completely out of your mind. Like 'a complete stranger' is what she said. Dilated eyes and all."

"So I was screaming for her to leave. What was I supposed to do?"

"Leave?"

"I did."

"But Aggie stayed. That gives me a clue as to who was in charge."

"You just don't get it, do you?"

"Did you tell her then that you didn't want her living on your property ever again?"

"Of course."

I point to the last page of the chapter Simone has been reading. "Aggie seemed to think that you were just in a mood, remember? You didn't make it clear that she wasn't working for you anymore. That you wanted her out of your life."

"I did my best, G.B."

"Apparently that wasn't enough."

Simone gives me that new searchlight look again, when her eyes throw out beams in two different directions. "It was enough," she says flatly. "More than enough."

"Well, it didn't do the trick, did it?"

Simone picks up the last page of my chapter and in a hoarse, wounded tone reads Aggie's last response: "'She...she told me to leave there...to leave and never come back...to just leave...and that you can't stay here another night, Aggie...yes..that's what she said...Aggie, you get out of here, do you hear me? You get out and you stay out. I didn't know...I had no idea...I...I can't....'" Simone drapes one arm over her eyes. "I had never seen Aggie cry before."

"Oh?"

"She wasn't the weeping willow type."

"Oh?"

"Oh? Oh? Is that all you can say?"

I shrug. "I'm listening."

"Listening for what?"

"Just listening."

"You know something, G.B.? I am, too. I'm beginning to hear voices," she says mysteriously. "At this point they're just whispering, and I don't quite know what they're saying. But they're friendly, and they're getting louder."

"What's that supposed to mean?" I ask, repressing a comment on schizophrenia. "What's your secret?"

Simone lifts the crook of her arm and one large brown eye focuses on mine. "You're the one acting secretive lately."

"Don't be ridiculous."

"Well, what then?"

"I'll tell you what." I sit down on the arm of the couch. "I've seen our collaborators every day this week, gone over the floorplan of the Marmottan with them a dozen times, gone to the Flea Market with Maggie to buy myself a fake I.D. and special license plates for Maggie's station wagon -- "

"Dirty old dull blue Renault -- "

"In which we'll look like a million other Frenchmen."

"With that crew? Fat chance!"

"I bought us five Magnums -- minus the ammo -- and a sturdy portfolio that will hold both *Sunrise* and *Sunset*."

"Blah, blah, blah."

"And while *Sunrise* waits for us in the trunk of our rental car, we'll leave the portfolio with *Sunset* -- "

Simone's voice-from-hell cuts me off with: "Somebody's gonna screw up."

"Here I have the heist all set for the last Sunday in

June. You have *Sunrise* almost finished. I have Part One of *The Deposition* mailed off already to old buddy Bob at Hutchins and Merrill. Why, we have the world at -- "

"My stomach." Simone hurls my manuscript across the room. "You're a real Jekyll and Hyde, you know that, G.B.?"

"I don't have to listen to this," I say, as I collect the pages. "Are you coming with me or not?"

"I'm sick, I tell you."

"It's just nerves. You can't be sick."

"Why can't I? You bought me that white leaded paint. Toxic, remember? And that tube of green arsenic -- "

"And I suppose you ate the red balloon?"

"I'm dying," moans Simone, "and what do you care? You'll get my money. It's all in your name. Take the money-"

"The Monet."

"And run off with that old flame. Paige Whatshername."

"Been there. Done that."

"When's the last time you heard from her? Bet the arsenic was her idea."

I slam the scrambled manuscript on the coffee table. "I've had it!"

"Yeah. You and Paige. In it together to poison me."

"She doesn't need your money."

"I suppose you've hidden your own assets."

"Sure. In a matchbox."

"Where's Paige living now? Around the corner?"

"Try the third floor," I growl. "Look. I give up with you. What do you want me to do? Tell the group the heist is off?"

"That group! How do you expect me -- or anyone -- to believe they're pulling this lark just for notoriety or nose-thumbing or whatever. It's fishy. Totally fishy. Just like your so-called novel."

"Okay, now I've really had it!" I can feel the blood

pounding in my temples. "The heist is off. We are off. I can be packed and out of here before dark. That suit you?" I glare at the white face on the couch. "You know what your trouble is, Simone? Developmental damage during childhood. And adolescence, too. Arrested development."

The minute I say this I regret it, seeing Simone's eyes droop from defiant Doberman to soppy Spaniel. I had a Cocker as a kid and never did get over the look Tippie gave me when I told him goodbye for the last time. It might just as well be Tippie looking at me now.

"Don't go, G.B."

"Don't go?"

"No. Stay. Please. And don't make me cling to your ankles as you head for the door like you told me Paige -- "

"Damn it, that wasn't Paige!"

"Okay, okay. I'm sorry."

"You've got to trust me."

Simone wipes her eyes with her fists. "Please stay."

"Come with me then." I go over to the couch and sit down on the arm again. "Nothing like the air of a June evening to work wonders for arsenic and old mace."

"Very funny."

"Come on." I pat her arm. "Let's get dressed."

"You told me to read the next chapter too," she whimpers.

"We'll take it with us."

Simone sighs. "Why do you always win?"

"Because I'm the omniscient narrator."

"Omniscient, hah!"

"What then?"

"The unreliable narrator."

I give her a kiss on each liquid eye. "That remains to be seen."

CHAPTER FIFTEEN

"There was this fellow coming out of the doggy door."

On the edge of the biggest bed in all Paris, I sit cross-legged, like the famous Egyptian Seated Scribe that Simone and I viewed the other day in the Louvre: back straight, hands resting on writing material in his lap, eyes front and center for all eternity. Perhaps he, too, was gazing at his mistress. The worshipful scribe. Ready to obey. Ready to write.

My own gaze is framed by our bathroom doorway and focuses upon Simone. She has rolled above her wrists the long sleeves of a ripe-plum blouse whose tails have been tucked into a pair of cream slacks. These now encase the curves of her derrière, perfectly, as seemlessly as the glass of a light bulb.

She is standing in front of her mirror and dressing table on which -- like offerings on an altar -- she has placed a tray of earrings from the black and gold Chinese lacquered chest that contains her treasury. In the mirror, the eyes of this mistress and scribe communicate.

With one forefinger, Simone caresses several of her jewels before she makes her choice. Her royal reflection smiles at me as she holds up a pair of Alexander Calder mobiles, in gold, black and plum. I nod. And the performance begins.

You would think the great Diaghilev himself had choreographed the exquisite movements that program Simone donning earrings. First the toss of her head that flicks a panel of her long chestnut hair back of one ear. Then, neck tilting, hips swaying, her hands lift the work of art to the lobe. Finally, the fingers gracefully guide the golden pin through that narrowest of tender orifices, in a subtle -- and enviable -- act of penetration. The second act follows: the penetration of the right earlobe as Calder's fortunate art becomes flesh, and flesh art. And I, breathless.

Simone again smiles at me in the mirror. She gives another tantalizing toss to her head, and wisps of hair nudge the earrings into life.

"Ah, sweet intoxication!" I say, dry-mouthed and starry-eyed. "Who thought the devil was clever when he held an apple out to Eve? He should have dangled a pair of earrings instead."

"Black opals?" suggests Simone. "Fire opals?"

"How much more succulent than fruit, the earlobe? How much more seductive, the affixing of the lure? This is what makes the beggar, what makes the beggar beg."

Simone dances by me and I reach out an arm.

"No," she commands. "Not now."

And I obey.

"You promised we were going out to some secret Valhalla of yours." She heads for the front door. "Coming?"

Yes, of course I'm coming. And I can wait. Oh yes, I can wait.

I next find myself trailing Simone along the quays by the Seine like a servant, breathing in her Rive Gauche perfume together with the river scents and the peculiar musty odors of the bookstalls that line the sidewalks. She eyes the old books; I eye Simone. And I am not the only one.

"Maybe a hundred years from now, G.B.," she turns to say, "your *Deposition* will be tucked away into one of these bookstalls, like all these Balzacs and Victor Hugos today."

"All the better to immortalize you."

"I could care less."

I have told her before about the obvious

incorrectness of that expression, but I can't help but say again, "You couldn't care less."

"Right."

I shrug. "Let's cross the Place Saint Michel." I point to the stoplight that has turned green.

"So where are we going?"

"Just going."

"Aggie again?"

I wave the roll of manuscript I am carrying. "We'll soon be done with her."

"Not soon enough."

We come to the corner of the Rue Saint Jacques and pause to admire Notre Dame Cathedral. Simone looks at it as if she has not moved for eight hundred years either.

"This street, by the way," I tell her, dragging her on, "is the old Roman Road that led Caesar's armies across the island and the Seine and on to England."

"Want me to take notes, Professor?"

"No need. Just keep your personal encyclopedia handy."

I steer Simone across the street and follow her through the little park next to the diminutive church of Saint Julien-le-Pauvre. The benches are filled this warm Sunday afternoon with parents keeping an eye on their screeching children, with lovers behaving as if there were no one around for blocks, and with loners looking to me like the song lyrics, 'Baby, the rain must fall.'

Simone suddenly jerks to a halt, and I plunge into her. Before I can complain, her dilated eyes direct my own to the rear of the park, to a corner bench white with pigeon droppings, where a bag lady is huddled over what was once a purse.

"Ccheezze," gasps Simone. "I thought it was Aggie."

"Don't you know that if Aggie were in Paris, she wouldn't be here?"

"Where would she be?"

107

"Changing the locks on our apartment door, of course!"

"I'm going home."

I stop Simone as she attempts to turn around. "Come on, lighten up. Why do you still let Aggie get to you like this?"

"Guilt?"

"That you could do without. And you soon will, when you see Aggie for who she really is. Come on." I propel Simone onward into the short, narrow Rue du Fouarre. "This was the heart of the old university quarter, when the Sorbonne was young -- in the thirteenth century."

"You sound like a tour guide. Where's your microphone?"

"You know why this is called the Latin Quarter?"

Simone begins moving her hips to some salsa beat coming from an upstairs window. "Lots of Latinos?"

"Latin. The language spoken by intellectuals in the Middle Ages."

"Well, pahhdon meeeee!" sniffs Simone.

"It was sort of like the Esperanto of the medieval era. All over Europe, educated people learned Latin as a second language. Then when they came here to lecture or study at the Sorbonne, they could all communicate."

"Got it."

"Right here, in the Rue du Fouarre, professors would lecture in Latin, and students would sit on bundles of straw. That's what Fouarre means -- an old word for straw."

"You are a real ambulatory Larousse, G.B."

By this time we have entered the Rue Dante, and I go on to mention that he, too, frequented the Latin Quarter. "In 1304, to be exact," I add.

"Probably rubbed shoulders with the young Countess Claire along about then," smirks Simone.

"I do my best to instill in you some sense of history, and you ignore it, like dime store candy. All you care about are the shapes and colors of things. Art and architecture -- the power of the line over the power of history, over the power of significant events."

"You got it!"

Simone sounds like Aggie, but I'm not going to tell her so. "History is observation, and observation gives perspective," I say instead. I wave my roll of manuscript again. "That's what I'm doing with this, too. Getting Aggie into perspective."

"Wait 'til I get you into perspective, G.B."

"Take your time," I tell her.

At the corner I take Simone's arm and bring us both to a halt. "We have arrived."

Simone looks up and across the street. "The Sorbonne? This is our secret destination? Been here. Seen that."

"But you haven't gone inside."

"Into the Great Inner Sanctum?"

"Yes." I nod, gazing with respect at the imposing building of the Sorbonne. "The Sanctum Sanctorum."

Simone genuflects dramatically and crosses herself.

We cross the street and she follows me as I walk reverently up the steps of my *alma mater* and inside, into the great hall.

Simone wrinkles her nose. "Stinks."

"It'll be awhile before they get a no-smoking ordinance here, I'm afraid."

"Smells of moldy old books, too."

"That's just your imagination." I guide Simone onward.

"I don't like it in here. It's spooky. I need fresh air."

"Later."

"Why were those doors unlocked, anyway?"

"To save Aggie the trouble?"

"Hohoho."

"Well, cleaning people may be working on a Sunday. And professors may be using their offices."

As if to validate my suppositions, a grey-haired gentleman in a rumpled three-piece suit, smoking a pipe and carrying a two-handled briefcase, appears before us from a side hallway. He tips his hat to us and saunters towards the entrance.

Simone sniggers. "Tipped his hat to us! Did you see that, G.B.? Who does that anymore? I feel like I'm in a time machine!"

I steer her onward down towards the end of the hallway and left into a smaller corridor. Then we come face to face with a set of double doors lettered: AMPHITHEATRE RICHELIEU.

I try a door handle and am pleased that it pushes open. "Where my lecture classes were held," I announce.

We step inside and Simone surveys the huge semicircular room, now silent and empty. Her eyes come to rest first on the battered desk that occupies the center of a raised platform in front of several feet of blackboard.

"I suppose the Great One sits on the stage?" Simone giggles. "Mouthing gobbledegook to all the dazed disciples sitting out there?" With that she waves an arm to indicate the rows of wooden straight-backed bench seats that rise in tiers in two layers, separated by the balcony railing.

"See the ladder over there?" I point across the room. "Like I said, they're probably cleaning here today."

"No windows?" is Simone's next observation.

"Only the windows of the intellect."

"Barf," coughs Simone. "Tell me, G.B., what good did any of those Great Ideas that flew around in here do any of you? Don't your intellectual giants turn out to be no better than village idiots? Arrogant idiots at that. You know what I think, G.B.?"

I am mesmerized by the Calder earrings that with a toss of Simone's head appear to be operating in four dimensions. All I can say is, "I can't imagine."

"What self-righteousness is to religious fanatics,

arrogance is to you and your intellectuals. Think about it."

"I will. Some other time." I take her hand and lead her around to the back of the amphitheater. "Let's go up to the peanut gallery."

We stumble up the dark stairs at the rear of the room and emerge into the balcony, walk down to the first row, center, and sit down. I take a deep breath, remembering all the heady lectures I witnessed from this very spot.

"This is like sitting on a rock," says Simone. "I'd rather be outside on a bale of straw." She shifts about in my silence. "Can we go now?"

"Not just yet."

"Floor's filthy. They need Aggie in here. She'd have it cleaned up in a jiff."

"I have Aggie right here." I remove the rubber band on the roll of manuscript I've been carrying. "I've dreamed of reading from my own writings right here in this room. Sort of like laying flowers on the altar."

"Say again?"

"I learned so much here."

"Like how to be a white-collar criminal?"

"How to examine people. Deconstruct them. See what makes them tick. Reveal them in all their nakedness."

"That's an art? Undressing Aggie?"

"Life imitates art."

"Life imitates farce."

I chuckle. "In Aggie's case, I have to agree."

"She did the best she could with what she had."

"You're beginning to sound like her attorney."

"Poor Calvin Carney was no match for P. Crawford Bennett."

Again, I chuckle. "But look what he had to work with. You work with a loser, you lose."

"Aggie may lose a few rounds, but she still comes out of her corner swinging."

"Swinging but losing."

"Don't bet on it, G.B. You know, Aggie's not really a bad person."

"You seem to be forgetting half the story. Like your truck?"

"I haven't forgotten."

"You and I had to take back your pick-up truck by force that December after Aggie had moved out. And then she stole it in January -- when you were up in Santa Barbara with me."

"She didn't steal it. She still had the keys. She had no transportation. And she needed it for Bubb-Bubb."

"Bubb-Bubb?"

"The name of our dog that had gotten torn up by a pit bull. Aggie had to take him to the vet." Simone frowns at me. "Don't you remember? It's all in her deposition."

"I know that. It was the week after you and I had loaded the truck with all Aggie's things and took them to some trailer park in Indio, where she had friends."

"Because she didn't want us to know where she was living."

"At any rate, in January Aggie was back at your home. Uninvited." I get to my feet. "And that's my cue. Time for my performance."

Simone squints up at me.

"Enjoy the show," I tell her.

I make my way back down the stairs, and the next Simone sees of me, I am walking down below her, down the main aisle towards the stage. In my head "Pomp and Circumstance" is playing, and Simone must hear it too because she applauds. But then, as I mount the platform, she gives me a crude wolf whistle. No matter. This is the moment I've been waiting for.

I locate the wall switch that turns on the microphone, flip it, then walk over to the desk and tap the mike. I test it with, "One, two, three, four -- "

"Ho, ho, it's Pussy Galore!" comes from the balcony.

"*The Deposition*," I announce. "Chapter Fifteen."

"Let's hear it: chapter and verse!"

"Aggie, as you know," I continue, as if the amphitheater were packed with eager students, "returns to Simone's house on foot with the intention of stealing her truck. When Mr. Bennett asks her if Simone had given her permission to use the truck she answers -- "

"You mean did she say, Aggie, use the truck?" is Simone's ad lib from the balcony.

I am quick to supply Mr. Bennett's question: "'Yes?'"

"No, she did not say, Aggie, use the truck."

I read Bennett's next question: "'Now, Mrs. Gretch, when you picked up the truck to go to the vet's, did you also enter the residence?'"

I glance up at the balcony, and Simone comes up with an astonishing near-verbatim Aggie: "I took the truck and took Bubb-Bubb up to Dr. Madson in Palm Springs, and he had to keep him to stitch up his leg, and I said, well, how long do you think it will be before you're done, Doctor? And he said, probably around noon and I said, I'll return. I wasn't ready to explain that all this was going on, 'cause he knew us, and so anyway, I was out in the street. I drove on over to Palisades Drive...and in all this confusion I was in at the time...and drove in the driveway and got out. The back gate was open and I heard a funny, funny kind of noise, and I went back to the truck and there was a stick in the back, and I grabbed that and I went around the corner of the house because I was still hearing this funny noise, and when I got around there, there was this fellow coming out of the doggy door."

"'What did he look like?'"

Simone doesn't miss a beat. "I can't explain him to you, Mr. Bennett," she says, "but he was a hippy-type fellow and I clobbered him on the back of the shoulder with the stick, and he scuffled along on the patio there, and he got out to the grass, and I had clobbered him a couple of times, and

113

when he hit the grass he got his footing and he got up and ran out the gate. I was running after him. He ran through the front yard and took off down Palisades Drive, and with that I had completely lost him, and I turned around and went back to the house thinking, my God, what is this now?"

"'How old was this guy, would you guess?'"

"I never saw his face, Mr. Bennett, because he was crawling out, and I hit him, and he had this long hair, and it was all down around his face anyway, and he got up and took off, and I only saw the back of the man, but I would judge he was in the twenties."

I am shaking with laughter and can hardly read my next line: "'What did this young man do when you hit him with a stick?'"

"He kept trying to get up, and he was rambling along the patio, and when he got his footing he was up and gone."

"'Did he attempt to hit you?'"

"No, he did not. He couldn't very well in a laying down position, Mr. Bennett, and when he got up he just ran."

"'Now after this alleged doggy door incident, did you yourself enter the residence?'"

"Me?"

"'You?'"

"Yes."

"'How?'"

"I went through the doggy door -- "

Here I have to interrupt Simone and say, "End of chapter."

With that, she leans over the balcony displaying a very full cleavage, laughs in an odd way, and beckons to me with a forefinger.

I rise to the occasion, my gaze riveted on the now frantic Calder mobiles that indicate a sense of urgency with which I can identify. There will be no shuffling up the backstairs for me. I stride over to the abandoned ladder, place it beneath the balcony railing, and as I mount the steps I hear a giggly:

"Dost thou love me, Romeo?"

"Ay, my Lady, more than thou canst know." With that, I clasp the balcony railing with both hands and with a strength I didn't know I had, vault up over the edge. I stand before her, flushed, and murmur: "A thousand times, hello!"

My lady begins unbuttoning her blouse. "Then take thy wanton Juliet."

And take her I do. Bench, railing, floor. On and about pieces of clothing strewn from one aisle to another. There we bang about with abandon. Until, that is, we hear a bass-baritone voice ascending the ladder, booming out in French what can be loosely translated as:

"Who put the fuckin' ladder out here?"

With that, a large grizzled head, apparently belonging to the voice, appears above the balcony railing. We are greeted by a pair of Breshnev eyebrows and wild eyes to match. And a huge flaccid mouth that has apparently lost the power of speech.

And so have both of ours.

Nothing to do but scramble for our clothes like frightened rabbits and hop for the dark stairway in the rear, there to cower until the workman's laughter has ceased and he has carried the ladder off to less interesting locales. Only then dare we exit the great Amphithéâtre Richelieu.

As we leave the Sorbonne -- our white and cream slacks now resembling soiled camouflage clothing -- I note that one of Simone's Calder mobiles looks twisted beyond repair. I dread what she will say when we get home and she sees herself in a mirror.

For the moment I try to lighten things up with, "Maybe we should have used the doggy door."

All Simone will say is, "Like I told you, G.B. Life imitates farce."

CHAPTER SIXTEEN

"Your girl friend here stuck you with the fork."

Sex, as everyone knows, is often even a bright person's undoing. But it won't be ours. After the incident at the Sorbonne yesterday, we made a solemn agreement: there will be no hanky-panky during the heist, tempting as that could be, given the two of us alone in the sous-sol of the Marmottan with Monet's *Sunrise* in our arms.

Simone, of course, took our *reductio ad absurdum* act in stride. She was needling me about other things over breakfast this morning. Namely about Aggie, and how reading that segment of my novel in "The Holy of Holies" -- as she put it -- amounted to nothing less than "The Canonization of Ella Agnes Gretch." Ridiculous! That's why I've left her alone in her studio most of the day while I finished Part Two of *The Deposition*, the last chapter of which is in my hand now as I cross the living room and enter Simone's own Sanctum Sanctorum.

She greets me with, "You know, G.B., the doggy door incident shows Aggie to be more creative than you. You copycat your material. She starts from scratch."

"I make scratch into literature. And besides, my engineering of the heist is more than creative. It's ingenious."

"If it works."

"It will work."

"As long as your moribund cohorts are still alive. Remember: the caper is still a week away."

I walk over to where Simone is doing her classic

hands-on-hips pose in front of her easel. The *Sunrise* that greets me is more than a pleasant surprise. "Brava!" I exclaim.

"A few touches on the frame." Simone squints at it, dabs at it, squints some more. Then announces: "It is finished."

I peer closely at her Monet now. "How you ever managed to do this, I will never understand."

"Well, remember when I had my fit?"

"Which one?"

"Very funny."

"The candlestick fit?"

"That was because I had put the drawing on the canvas and then I was trying to add the orangey background and that didn't work, like, Monet painted the underpainting with a horizon line and the sky and the water first, fast, and then he added all that blue murk, boom-boom-boom" -- here Simone's right arm flails about -- "and the smokestacks, zoop-zoop-zoop-zoop." Both arms flail here. "Well, screw the line drawing on the canvas! Because I got this brilliant idea to take a perfect photograph instead, make a slide, and, after I had done all the underpainting, project the slide on the canvas and outline basically all the contained areas like the form of the murky areas, and then, within that outline, make my strokes spontaneously."

Obviously, Simone is talking in tongues again. And she has the nerve to refer to much of contemporary literary criticism as gobbledegook! But in the spirit of the moment I tell her good-naturedly, "It's all sleight of hand to me."

"So what about your own magic trick? Which, I might add, has nothing magical about it."

"You superimpose a slide projection to perfect your Monet, and I use a legal deposition to get my own right. Same thing. Mine's finished, too. All but the Appendix. Time for you to read the last chapter."

"What could top the doggy door incident?"

117

"The pitchfork episode?"

"It was a strawfork."

Who the hell cares is what I'm thinking as I take Simone's arm, and we walk back into my studio and sit down on the couch. "You remember where we left off?" I ask. "When Mr. Bennett asked Aggie about going inside the house via the doggy door?"

"You're asking me? How Aggie kept ranting on and on about that hippy who had one bolt almost out of the bottom hinge and was trying to spring it when she caught him in the act and clobbered him?"

"And Aggie finally had to admit that she went inside to hide some of your jewelry, so that I, 'evil Eva,' wouldn't spirit it away. Also had the nerve to leave a note by the kitchen sink."

"She wanted to make sure I knew that my swimming pool wasn't working right -- that the gasket wasn't circulating, and the filter basket was broken."

"Aggie also had the nerve to paw through our garbage and tell your friends that the trash was full of empty wine bottles, all my fault, of course."

Simone heaves a mighty sigh. "What's the sense in all this rehashing?"

"Think of it as a woman's quest novel."

"Tell me what possible quest there is in your sleazy *Deposition.*"

"The quest for truth. What other quest is there?"

"The quest for identity."

"Granted. But that's a form of truth, too. Besides, Aggie must be exorcised. Or at least taken down from her cross."

Simone giggles. "Another deposition! That makes three!"

"You are cleverness itself." I give Simone a congratulatory kiss on the cheek. "And speaking of quest novels, think of Hemingway -- "

"A macho jerk!"

"But oh, could he write!"

"Men like that won't let a woman be, so how can she have a quest?"

"You mean they create an ontological block to prevent women from Be-ing?"

"Yes, professor, and you can hold the gobbledegook. That is exactly what I mean. Out to delude, limit, intimidate women, and you know why? Hemingway and millions like him are scared to death of a liberated woman!"

"You've come a long way, Baby -- "

"Don't turn me off."

"Okay, okay, let's get back to Aggie."

"Back to your farce? Like you getting me to phone the police to tell them that Aggie had stolen my truck and run off with my jewelry, all of which netted her a thirty-thousand dollar bail on her head. And she hadn't done anything, really."

"Really!" I snort, more than surprised at Simone giving her blessing to Aggie's illicit actions.

"Well, she showed that Deputy Ramsfeld where my jewelry was hidden. And she eventually returned the truck. And she did get all her things off my property."

I could comment on what I sense is a betrayal of sorts, but instead I hold up the last chapter of my manuscript and say, "And that brings us to the final scenes."

At no suggestion from me, Simone begins reading, and I along with her:

Q. Now, Mrs. Gretch, let's go back to the doggy door incident. What items did you remove from Simone's home at that time?

A. I took some antiques that I had felt belonged to me, and I later returned them to Simone because she told me over the phone that she wanted them and that they belonged to her, and I said, well, Baby, you can have anything you want.

Q. What else?

A. A few pictures off the wall. Some tools.

Q. Anything else?

A. Mr. Bennett, everything there's in such a confusion at that time in my life, I didn't know exactly the things I took that day, other than things that were mine, or I felt were mine, or that I needed. With the things that I have now, I'm not completely sure. Maybe if someone was to say, Aggie, did you take so and so, you know, when Simone kicked me out. I still don't know what I have and don't have.

Q. Are you claiming now that you have personal property at Simone's residence?

A. How could I know what all, with her and Eva refusing to let me in to pack my own things, saying how dangerous I was. There's so many things that I can't even recall, and my mind being foggy and all, but rocks I'd collected. Rocks in the garden there that belong to me, wood I stacked there, and a bolt of material that the Tinkles gave me. You can ask them.

I have to giggle. "Like that's what you'd really want to keep -- some old bolt of material."

"I have no idea what happened to it. I really don't."

"Hey! I'm not accusing you, remember?"

"And Aggie thought I had her butane camp stove, and her camping gear, too. She must have given it all away."

"You calling Aggie generous?"

"She'd give you the shirt off her back."

"Ugh! I wouldn't want it."

Again, without any urging on my part, Simone continues reading, as do I:

Q. Now then, Mrs. Gretch, there is attached to the complaint you filed a document which is entitled "Tentative Agreement to be finalized as of December 20, 1983." Are you familiar with that?

A. I ought to be.

Mr. Carney: *Yes or no, Aggie.*

A. Yes.

BY MR. BENNETT:

120

Q. This is a typewritten document, marked "Exhibit B." Who typed this?

A. Simone or Eva, one of them had to, because they were the only people there that day.

Q. What day?

A. The day they typed it up.

I burst out laughing again. "Aggie is a gem! You know something? When I finish with this *Deposition*, I'm going to miss her."

Simone gives me a dreamy, "Me, too."

We read on:

Q. Tell me what happened that December day when Simone handed you the Agreement.

A. I was there at the time, to try to talk with Simone, and she told me to take my stuff and leave and so forth, and that thing they had typed up, that she handed me, said that she would give me the truck and that she would give me $1500 in cash too, if I was to have everything out by midnight on Christmas Eve.

Q. Did she, in person, hand you this document?

A. Yes, she did.

Q. What did she say when she handed it to you?

A. "Here."

This time I double over with laughter. "'Here!'" I repeat. "'Here!'"

Simone is silent, already reading the next page. I catch up with her:

Q. By Christmas Eve of 1983, Mrs. Gretch, did you get all of your property out of Simone Franklin's residence?

A. Not hardly.

Q. No?

A. Like I said, they wouldn't let me in to pack up.

Q. May I remind you that you're under oath?

A. I am telling the truth, the whole truth, and nothing but the truth, so help me God. You just can't seem to understand what I went through with this girl. She -- she didn't want to talk to me. She had no idea of what she was getting into with Eva. All I wanted was to talk. Wanted to help before it was too late. You have no idea, Mr. Bennett, what that schemer Eva could get Simone into before --

Q. Mrs. Gretch --

A. That day I said hello, Simone, Baby, I --

Q. Okay, Mrs. Gretch --

A. Simone, Baby, I said, I've got to talk to you. She didn't want to talk to me. All I wanted was to talk. Wanted to help. Simone, I said, I've just got to talk to you. And she --

I look at Simone to share a smile and can't believe what I see: a tear running down her cheek. She quickly brushes it away and looks up at the ceiling. I decide to proceed without comment.

"This is where Bennett asks Aggie what occurred that January day when she was to load up all her things down at the burned-out building and get off your property once and forever. When -- "

"It was your idea, G.B., for us to offer to help her. Use my truck. Get it all packed up. I thought that was good of you at the time, but now I know you had other motives."

"I did?"

"One way to make sure it was all out. And fast."

"Shall we let Aggie tell it? When Bennett asks her what occurred?"

Simone doesn't answer but reads:

A. Well, I still had stuff I had stored down there and Simone and Eva had determined that I was to take it. That I should remove it all one day, last of January I think it was, and they would help me in the truck. Because there wouldn't be any other time to get the stuff. Like, they weren't inconveniencing themselves at any other time. And I should get my friend Jarvis Tinkle to take me to meet them down there and they'd follow us then in the truck to take my stuff home.

Q. Did that, in fact, happen?

A. I said no, I couldn't do that, because Deputy Ramsfeld had advised me not to let them know where I was living. So I told them they could load it and follow me over to Mr. and Mrs. Tinkle's trailer and unload it there in the yard.

Q. And did Mr. Tinkle go with you?

A. Yep, sure did. Jarvis went with me and when Simone and Eva finally got there, Simone unlocked the door to the building, which they had padlocked, and we went inside.

Q. Did anything occur out of the ordinary?

"Out of the ordinary!" squawks Simone. "Tell me one thing that occurred that was ordinary! When I think about it today, it seems like I must have been sleepwalking."

"Sleepwalking through your prison bars."

Simone gives me a long look I cannot deconstruct. I point to the page with Mr. Bennett's question about out of the ordinary, and say, "This is the best part of the whole novel."

Reluctantly, Simone's eyes follow mine, and we read on:

A. Well, Jarvis helped with the heavy stuff and I'd got most of my things out and then Simone and I went back into the building alone. I had reached up on the wall to get...well, she calls it a pitchfork, but it wasn't, it was a strawfork, and Simone said, what are you doing with that? And I said, I would like to borrow it and clean up my yard. And she said no, you can't. And I said Simone, come on, let me use the fork. And she said you can't use anything on this property. And I say, okay, Baby, and started to put the fork back up where it came from, on the rack, and with that Eva burst in the door and said Simone, you're not staying in here with that crazy woman with the pitchfork in her hand. And with that I said Eva, I have been with Simone for fifteen years and I never put a hand on her or would. Now with you it's a different story. And then she came after me and I stepped back, and I had the fork in front of me, and she grabbed the handle and with that we whirled around a couple of times, and I said for God's sake, stop this. Someone's going to get hurt. And she was doing her best to get the fork away from me, but I wasn't about to surrender it so she could stick me with it. So when I whirled around the last time I was with my back to the side door, and Simone, in the scuffle, had backed up into these tools on the wall, and the stuff on the floor, and with that I said Eva, and just as I said Eva, Eva made a jump with the fork and held it like this, and it went up there, and I had moved in front of Simone in the scuffle, and with that, Eva let it down quick, and pushed again, and one of the prongs punched Simone in the leg and she screamed, see what you've done, Aggie! You stuck me in the leg with the fork! And I said, your girl friend here stuck you with the fork! And with that I let go of it and went outside and Jarvis said, Aggie, what is happening? And I said well, I don't know, I really don't.

With that, I burst out laughing. "That was the wildest dance I've ever done!"

"You may laugh now, but you were acting crazy then. You looked like you could have killed Aggie."

"She could have killed you!"

"No way. She's all bark and no bite. You saw how she went to pieces at the end of her deposition."

"You don't think that was fake?"

"No, G.B. That wasn't fake."

I could argue with that, but instead I say, "You're looking at me as if you hate me."

Simone holds up the last page of my chapter. "This is it?"

I nod, irritated that she hasn't responded to my allegation of hate. "Here's where Bennett concludes -- "

"Yes, yes. And Aggie signs the deposition, declaring under penalty of perjury that her testimony is true and correct. And Sally S. Smock, certified reporter and notary public, witnesses that the deposition is a true record of the testimony. Signed, sealed, and certified. Blah, blah, blah."

"March 3, 1984. I'll sign for Sally. Would you like to sign for Aggie?"

"You're the one that needs to be certified, G.B." Simone leans her head on the back of the couch and closes her eyes. "Q. and A., Q. and A.," she groans. "I'm so sick of Q. and A. -- "

"Then let's turn a page of another kind."

Simone opens one eye that follows my movements as I get up off the couch and go over to the window. There I pose socratically, arms folded, as I look out over the Seine, thinking I could live here forever and a day.

"What are we going to do about the landlady?" I ask. "She phoned again this morning. She really does want to sell this apartment." I turn around and face Simone, who has both eyes open now. "Are you still interested?"

"Why not?"

"This will be a permanent home for *Sunrise* then?"

"Always thinking up new schemes, aren't you, G.B.?"

"The French have the perfect expression for it: a *ménage à trois.*" I go back to Simone. "Sunday is the Big Day. When we bring the Baby home."

"Either that or we will go directly to jail -- "

"And not collect our $200?"

"Always playing games," mumbles Simone.

"Monopoly was one of my favorites."

"Bet your little Dickie Halloway was no match for you."

"You're right," I smile. "I always won."

Simone's eyes are hooded now, and her voice comes from-nowhere when she says, "Maybe it's my turn to win."

CHAPTER SEVENTEEN

"Here come da judge!"

It is D Day: Sunday, June 30, 1985. But first of all, let me mention in passing that Simone and I rented a Renault Le Car on Friday for the week-end. Yesterday morning we drove out to Giverny to see -- for the fifth time -- Claude Monet's house and gardens, which Simone enters with more reverence than she offers any of the great cathedrals of Europe. We were back home early in the evening, however, and early to bed, because today was to begin at five in the morning. That is an hour that does not usually find us up and sucking espresso. Certainly not Simone, whose resources permit lingering between the sheets until noon. (Or throughout the entire afternoon, for that matter, should the preceding evening warrant it.)

It is now five-thirty and we are already back in Le Car -- a red one, by the way, due to the rental agency's mistake, and not at all our idea of passing unnoticed -- and driving out to the Bois de Boulogne. I park it in an inconspicuous spot near the Lac Inférieur, as the Lower Lake in the woods is called. As I roll up the windows and lock the doors, Simone has to kick one red fender and launch her Parthian shot: "We're supposed to be invisible in this siren? Might as well be driving a tank!"

I ignore the remark. Acknowledging her emotional wind-up at this point could pitch the whole scene into histrionics.

Clutching our portfolio -- which, needless to say, contains Simone's *Sunrise* -- I lose no time in marching her

126

out of the Bois to the nearest métro entrance, Muette. Our destination is across town, at Denfert-Rochereau, a stop just a block from Maggie's quarters on the Boulevard Saint-Jacques.

We climb the single flight of stairs to her apartment and knock. The door opens, and there stands Maggie, a pith helmet crushed down over her ears and resting on her vintage spectacles, just about three inches above a portion of salt and pepper mustache pasted on her left upper lip. Simone -- and this is at seven on a Sunday morning -- gives out with one of her most godawful screeches. Why neighbors do not appear in doorways or phone the French equivalent of 911 can be explained only by imagining the riotous atmosphere which must, as a rule, prevail in the space in and around Maggie's apartment.

Its interior is a smoke-filled disaster area which even Simone calls cluttered. But the walls are colored with priceless paintings. Most of them are askew, and all of them dusty, but each one was a gift from the artist: Matisse and Miro, Georges Braque, Picasso and Juan Gris, to name a few. All friends from Maggie's cubist period.

Simone deserves the nasty poke in the ribs I give her when she breaks into a laughing-coughing fit over the wigs being slipped on by the chihuahua and the greyhound, as Simone now constantly calls Céline and Countess Claire: a Tootsie blond one for the chihuahua, and jet black frizzy tresses for the greyhound who, with her heavy red lipstick and gray shift, makes a ghastly caricature of Mortitia of Addams Family fame.

Maggie -- quite an expert at stage make-up from her theater days off Broadway -- has beards and mustaches for both Simone and me, hers chestnut and mine dark chocolate and rather good matches for our hair, which we tuck up under baseball caps. Also for us are somewhat rumpled but fairly presentable men's suit pants and sports jackets -- Simone's labeled NBA and mine Raiders -- with enough padding in them to make us each look twenty pounds heavier

127

and, with the added facial hair, a good ten years older.

"Outrageous!" pronounces Simone.

"Then you have probably never been to Amsterdam or Istanbul, Cairo or Calcutta either, for that matter," Maggie tells her. "Not to mention that world-class mecca for transvestites: the Castro in San Francisco."

Even Simone has no reply for that one.

While we are admiring ourselves in the hall mirror, an imperious knock at the door announces Margo Duc. She has just driven into Paris from her country estate and is, as she puts it, in high drag: spike heels, an immaculate black skirt suit, black gloves, and a splendid string of pearls with earrings to match. Simone, of course, has to blurt out a brassy, "Here come da judge!"

But the Judge is unflinching. She pounces upon Simone with that 'Well, hello hello again!' look in her yellow cat eyes. She sweeps an arm around Simone's waist and has kisses planted on both of her cheeks -- calculatedly close to the corners of the mouth -- before I can intercept with a distancing handshake. Then, all swish and flappy arms, Margo does a nelly-queen flight around the room, complimenting Maggie en route on her baggy pin-striped suit, and the pair of dilapidated tennis shoes that barely protrude from the pantlegs.

We leave the apartment at exactly ten past nine. As I wonder how the six of us are escaping virtually unnoticed by other tenants and passers-by, I can only imagine what an incredible parade these lucky people must have become accustomed to over the years.

Back out on the Boulevard Saint-Jacques, Simone and I slip our portfolio into the trunk of Maggie's station wagon without anyone else realizing that it is suspiciously heavy. We then take our seats: the Judge alongside Maggie in the front, Simone and I in the rear, and the dogs in the middle.

Sadly, the old wagon won't start. Simone slumps over in her seat, babbling incoherently. But out pops the Judge, whipping off her black gloves and rolling up her coat sleeves. Under the hood she dives, telling all the while she pulls spark plug wires and removes the distributor cap of how she drove alone in 1938 from Shanghai to Ulan Bator in Outer Mongolia. How she ran out of oil, stopped a caravan of nomads, bought sheep and had them slaughtered, and fed the multitudes before she melted the animal fat, poured it into the engine, and drove off.

"Hand me a screwdriver, Maggie," comes the voice from under the hood.

While Maggie rummages through her jam-packed junk-packed glove compartment, a bakery van pulls up alongside us and an elderly man gets out. With his bald head and gigantic white mustache, he looks just as oddly disguised as we.

"*Je peux vous aider, Madame?*" he asks the Judge in cavalier fashion, at the same time throwing Maggie a faint male-bonding look. We all know that their disguises, at least, are working.

I can see Margo opening her mouth to say "*Non,*" but then thinking better of it, remembering her Sunday role. She lets him take the screwdriver that Maggie is dangling out the window, smiles demurely and sighs, "*Oh, merci, Monsieur! Mille fois merci!*"

Whatever he does, it works. The motor turns over and off we speed, Maggie driving like a maniac now to make up for precious lost minutes.

And, I must say, I am wide-eyed with admiration for her, handling that old wagon as if it were James Bond's latest BMW. That is, until we hit the Boulevard Périphérique -- the expressway system that encircles Paris. That's when Maggie suddenly turns her neck to check for traffic in the slow lane with which our entrance ramp is merging and in so doing bangs her pith helmet against the side window. As we zoom out onto the freeway, the helmet clamps down over her left eye at a forty-degree tilt and sends her cigarette and vintage glasses flying.

Fortunately, Maggie is able to follow the blur ahead until a relatively safe space develops behind a giant furniture truck. By that time the Judge has managed to retrieve the cigarette -- which has burned an ugly hole in Maggie's pantleg -- and the glasses. They now have a crack in one lens, but nevertheless put the world back into focus for our driver. All of the above is not without a sly and prolonged "Ooo, la, la!" from Margo in reference to Maggie's legs -- not what they once were, perhaps, but then again, not what they would one day become, either.

The entire scene sends the greyhound howling and the chihuahua yipping with a fury. Simone simply puts her hands over her eyes and sways back and forth like an autistic child.

I am speechless with terror.

CHAPTER EIGHTEEN

*"Reason is like a frayed G-string that
can no longer cover the essentials."*

It is not long after the Judge retrieved Maggie's glasses
and cigarette. Now she has launched into some detailed tale
of seduction that allegedly took place during the rainy season
in Acapulco.

"This girl was the most gorgeous armful you could
ever imagine," she croons. "Chocolate almond eyes, creamy
skin, cherry nipples -- "

"Sounds like a hot fudge sundae," Simone interrupts,
in a flat tone that indicates an ashen state of mind.

"Good enough to eat, too," the Judge goes on,
unperturbed. "Uneducated, according to our standards, but
deliciously naive. All imagination. Like when I asked her her
name and she said, 'Tan-ya.' Tanya? I repeated. Tania? With a
Y or an I? The girl's eyes became wonderfully glazed,
reaching deep into inner space for an answer. Then she
smiled confidently, looked straight into my eyes and said,
'No. With a T.'"

Titters all around. Except for Simone's "Shhiiiitt!"

My elbow in her rib cage goes by unacknowledged.
That tells me she is tuning up for a good one. She plunges
into it with: "Why is it that so many of you macho
intellectuals -- male or imitation male -- take such delight in
carrying on with your inferiors?"

I jockey into position and give her a really painful
poke in the ribs. "Stop that," she tells me in her
no-uncertain-terms voice. "Why?" she repeats, louder this

131

time. "Do you want to know? Know why you don't get someone on your own level?"

"My dear," the Judge replies without a feather out of place, "I've had them on all levels."

More titters all around.

Simone leans forward, between the dogs' heads. "It's so you can feel superior, that's why. Nothing like hanging around some foolish uneducated female to blow up a deflated macho ego. Look at that snool Rousseau."

"You are referring to Jean-Jacques, my dear?" (This from the wan Countess, who has paled -- if such a thing were possible -- at Simone's impending sacrilege.)

"Just look at what the jerk did! Lived with a laundress, as I recall."

Here Simone looks at me for verification, her reference coming from one of my lectures she attended at Santa Barbara. I pretend invisibility, wishing I were anywhere but next to her in the back of Maggie's stock-car, hell bent for the Marmottan.

Simone plows ahead. "Your great Rousseau used her like a servant all his life. Had what, four or five kids from her, and abandoned them all on the church doorstep like a thief in the night. Which he was. Lived off women and lived on lies, all the while mouthing equality. What a dickhead!"

"Really, my dear," comes from the Countess.

"Yes, really, my dears. Surely you've read *La Nouvelle Héloïse*."

"I assure you we have read ~~everything~~ Jean-Jacques ever wrote." (This again from the Pale One.)

I begin sweating profusely as the hostilities escalate. I can't believe Simone can be blowing the heist like this. But there is no stopping her now.

"Look at Rousseau's two separate tracks of education -- one for females, one for males. One for the masters, one for the slaves. Role separation: divide and conquer. Make sure the men will run things and the women will obey. Any idiot can see it. How could you worship him and pretend to be feminists? Talk about a bunch o' crock -- "

"You do have a point there." (This from the Judge.)

"The Great Guérillères? Preaching freedom from the patriarchy? Cutting a caper like today's just to embarrass some members of the old Phallic State?"

Members? I could run with that one, but I beg: "Please -- "

"Oh, I know, in the Really Great Days of Yore you were a pack of revolutionaries. But those days are over. What we need today are real radicals. Of the color red, not beechwood. That's what you are. Beachwood people. Washed out. Washed up. Yesterday's feminists."

"Enough, Simone," I say. "Apologize to these women. You've no reason to behave with such foul manners here."

Simone slumps back in her seat. "All right, all right. I'm sorry I had to say all that, but it's true. And yes, I do have foul manners, and I'm ignorant, and I have no degrees." Then she glares at me. "And I am so small, as Aggie would say, that I could crawl under a snake's belly."

"Oh, please, don't drag Aggie into it."

"But I do know this: most of the so-called literature you carry on about is written by men wiping their feet on women. Keeping house with their inferiors and keeping them inferior. And telling them what sweet little cutie pies they are to stay in their places."

"Really, my dear!" (This, of course, from the Countess.)

"And Maggie, your pal André Breton making use of mad Nadja for -- "

"I never could stand that man," snaps Maggie, lighting yet another cigarette. "Thought he was God's gift."

"Don't you agree, though," I say, leaning forward between the dogs now myself and projecting my remarks to the front of the wagon, "that Breton is, nevertheless, a

133

monument to twentieth century literature for having established the primary importance of the irrational in the creative process?"

"Blah, blah, blah." (So saith Simone.)

Relieved that she is side-tracked, at least, I forge right ahead. "The right hemisphere. That's what Sartre and his ilk never understood."

"Yeah, yeah." (Simone at it again.)

"All trying to apprehend reality rationally. Not realizing that reason is like a frayed G-string that can no longer cover the essentials."

"Now where have I heard that one?" smirks Simone. She recognizes it, of course, from my fake doctoral dissertation.

"Reality is like life," I add, especially for her benefit. "It has no rational plot."

Céline blows us a garlic-tinged puff of air with a jerk of her head, signifying Freudian-Sartrian disagreement. I can't resist adding, "And Robbe-Grillet and the so-called New Novelists missed the point, too."

"Absolutely," the unruffled Judge agrees.

"An absolute failure, a ridiculous, childish attempt to present the direct experience of an observerless world. Now that's really laughable." And here I laugh. "Trying to produce an I-less mode of perception that is so I-filled -- "

Simone cuts me off with a howling, "Oh, no, no, no, no!"

"What's the matter now?" I ask her coldly, severed from what might have been one of my finest speeches.

"Did I turn the bathroom heater off before we left the apartment?"

"I don't believe you, Simone. Every damned time we leave home it's something. Did I shut the oven off? Did I unplug the iron? Did we lock the door? And just when we get too far away to go back. It never fails."

Simone's response: moans.

"You never think of it half a block from home."

Her response: more moans and "I can't remember."

"Compulsive behavior," barks the Freudian chihuahua.

"Well, it's too late now," I snap at Simone. "We're not turning back. You'll just have to forget about it."

Simone bites her lower lip and turns her head towards the window to pout.

"What's happening, Aggie?" I ask, trying to lighten things up. No answer.

"Let's go back to the novel," the Judge suggests. "Where do you think it's going from here?"

"Nowhere," states Full Professor Céline Chantefable, winner of academe's highest awards, one-time editor of the prize-winning collection of conference papers entitled *'Pseudonymity in the Poetic Nexus: Studies in the Ideologies of Autotelic Art.'* "Tomorrow's novel is in a cul-de-sac."

"Psychobabble," snorts Simone.

"The novel is most certainly not at the end of its tunnel," I say, thinking of my own *Deposition*. Before I know it I have stepped on the chihuahua with my own professorial (German shepherd) voice: "It's the critics who have nowhere to go."

"Today's novel is just a buffer zone of words," Céline spits back, wounded to the quick, of course. "A forgery."

The word "forgery" stops my tongue as well as my racing heart, and Simone and I trade guilty looks.

The Judge turns around and picks me out with her cat eyes. "Tunnel, you said. I see the novel as a sort of dark tunnel at the end of the senses, illuminated only by words. A flicker here, a flicker there, here a dim light, there a blinding light -- "

"RED LIGHT!" Simone and I both yell as Maggie sails off the exit ramp and out into the busy Avenue de Saint Cloud. Six necks snap as she slams on the brakes.

When we have come to a full stop, Maggie turns

around slowly and from beneath her pith helmet targets us all in a thin, horizontal gaze. Then she says very quietly, very properly, "Shut up. All of you."

We do.

CHAPTER NINETEEN

"This whole fucked-up job."

A few minutes later we pull up at the Marmottan. It is exactly two minutes past ten, and the museum has just opened. Miraculously enough, we are right on schedule.

We synchronize our watches one last time while we wait until the short line of visitors at the entrance all have their tickets and are safely, so to speak, inside. Maggie decides to take no risks with the old Renault and to keep the engine running until we return, a projected thirteen minutes from now.

"Okay, ladies," I say, slipping into my wrap-around sunglasses, "straight ahead!"

Simone and I go in first. We calmly buy our tickets and wait briefly for our three companions to do likewise, and for the area to clear of tourists. Then we pull out our guns, empty of ammunition of course, and quietly take over the entrance. We seat the two museum officials in chairs at a nearby desk and leave the Countess (the "Cuntess" as Simone has begun to call her) standing guard over them. Since the museum alarm system can be set off only near the entrance, by taking over that area immediately we have a *laissez-passer* to the entire museum.

Simone and I head downstairs. There we assemble the three unarmed guards and about a dozen tourists into a ragged platoon and flush them up the stairs. A moment later Céline and the Judge appear in the corridor, escorting the other six guards and another dozen or so visitors from the

137

main and upper floors. We herd the whole frieze-faced flock into the room of miniatures. Everything is working to perfection.

And then Simone gasps. There is the Judge, in those tense and fearful circumstances, taking a precious moment out to pat the *derrière* of one of her prisoners and whisper some sweet nothing in her ear! There you have it. Power, money, fame, plot...they all pale in the dark light of lust. The kiss of undoing, the perilous caress, the no matter what the cost embrace...they turn us all into brainless puppets willing to forfeit everything for a breath of ecstasy.

The woman is spectacular, I must say, in a crisp rust linen skirt-suit and heels, a knotted chocolate and matching-eye blue scarf at her throat. But she turns and gives the Judge a look that you could skate on in hell. Even ol' lemon eyes moves off with the chill, while Simone -- noting my tethered eyes -- sticks me in the ribs with her pistol and snarls, "Move!"

I move.

At the museum entrance I hand the Countess my Colt for safekeeping and hurry out to the station wagon. The engine is still running, and behind the wheel Maggie is almost invisible under her pith helmet. I carefully lift the portfolio out of the trunk.

Back inside, Simone and I fly downstairs. We depose *Sunset*, then *Sunrise*, and hang our original in its place. With the two Monets in our portfolio, we race back upstairs.

Céline is escorting the last two arrivals at the Marmottan into the room for lock-up. They are a middle-aged, stoic Russian couple who had entered the museum only to be taken into custody by our Countess. Hearing their accents, she was no doubt reminded of doing time in KGB prison camps. Only that could explain the obscene pleasure she appears to take in waving her gun under their noses and growling at them in Lithuanian.

The prisoners are told to stay put until ten forty-five,

at which time they can simply open the door, phone the police, go have a drink or two, or go to church and give thanks for the happy ending to their Sunday morning adventure. Or go visit some other museum. (The Judge's instructions and suggestions, beautifully stated in both French and English.)

At exactly twenty-one past ten, six minutes late, we all climb back into the station wagon, where Maggie is revving the engine. I can hear the radiator gurgling.

"I suppose it's going to boil over right here and now," Simone has to whine. "And in the next chapter we'll be in the pokey."

Hot engine or no, we lurch away from the curb and peel rubber down the diminutive Rue Louis-Boilly, which runs perpendicular to and ends abruptly in the large and busy Boulevard Suchet. In seconds we have gathered space-shuttle speed and are all six screaming in unison. Maggie's dilapidated tennis shoe -- or, rather, the tear over the little toe on the right foot -- has caught on the accelerator. (The "exhilarator," as Simone used to say, before I undertook responsibility for her education.)

The Judge dives once again for the floor -- no one thinking to turn the key off in the ignition -- and manages to free the anchored sneaker just as we shoot straight across the Boulevard. Who knows how the wagon slips magically in between clusters of cars? Not I. My eyes are tightly closed as I scream my farewell to planet earth.

But then Maggie's foot hits the brake pedal, and we jolt up over the curb on the far side of the Boulevard and plunge into a tiny park marked by a sign that reads: "*Square des Ecrivains Combattants Morts pour la France.*" Square of Writers Who Fought and Died for France? A guffaw dies in my stomach as we fishtail across the gravel, somehow missing flower beds and benches and a bug-eyed poodle with its bug-eyed keeper. All much to Maggie's credit -- she who learned to drive in the thirties with the great French novelist

139

Blaise Cendrars in his legendary Bugatti.

We finally come to rest near the far end of the Square, next to another sign. This one reads: "*Interdit aux chiens même tenus en laisse.*" Forbidden to dogs, even on leashes? That does it! I blow apart in uncontrollable laughter, all the more hysterical given the icy silence of the others.

Meanwhile, Maggie -- now in full control of the old Renault-- jolts us over another curb and points the wagon down the Avenue du Maréchal Maunoury. Got to give her credit. Lots of it.

"You're going to pay for this," Simone lets me know, as we head for the Bois de Boulogne.

"Pay?"

"Yes, Mrs. Gretch, pay."

"For what?"

"This whole fucked-up job."

"I still haven't figured out why you joined up with us in the first place," the Judge says kindly to Simone. "You have nothing to gain from all this, right?"

"Wrong," states Simone, in her cool-hand-Luke voice.

"Careful," I whisper.

The Judge winks at her. "Well, I certainly wouldn't have missed it. Did you notice that knock-out in the rust suit?" Another lemon wink, this one aimed at me, even though I am doing my very best to be invisible. "Steely on the surface," she goes on, "sultry down deep. You can bet on it."

"I find your ruling questionable, Judge," hisses Simone. "Your *femme fatale* looked like the kind of bitch that would chew a mouthful of people thirty-two times before swallowing -- ouch!" I have given Simone a good poke in the ribs, but it doesn't silence her. "And as for her mind, I bet you could travel all through it in just no time at all."

With this, she snaps her fingers, loudly, and right behind the dogs' ears. They both flinch, and I give Simone another poke, harder this time, and she pokes me back, harder yet.

140

"And what is more ridiculous than some imitation-macho-male dyke who thinks that one good screw'll tame any shrew?" Simone goes on in something of a semi-shriek. "You're missing what New Feminism is all about."

Oh, no, I think to myself. Not that again! I may live by my wits, but I am about at wits' end.

A linguistic commotion follows. A bilingual cacophony that clatters on until Maggie interrupts with another no-nonsense "Shut up!" In spite of all the spitfire and self-inflicted terrorism, she has managed to find the precise spot where I told her I had parked our Le Car. Kudos.

We pull up alongside it in silence and Maggie switches off the motor. More ominous gurgles come from under the hood. Maggie is unruffled. "Now," she says, calmly and grandly, as if she were addressing guests at a Cape Cod charity ball, "now let me invite you to a drink." From beneath the driver's seat she retrieves a silver liter flask, unscrews the plug and asks, ever so politely, "Who'll be first?"

"You!" We are simultaneous and unanimous in our vote, forgetting that Maggie is, so to speak, on the wagon.

After a long, leisurely draught, Maggie pronounces it the best Russian vodka she has ever tasted. Barring, of course, the bottle Blaise Cendrars once brought her from St. Petersburg.

"Blaise was never in St. Petersburg," mumbles the Chihuahua in the greyhound's ear.

Maggie seems not to hear and passes the flask around, and we all drink our fill. Even the dogs, although with raised eyebrows at partaking from such a collective trough. Our tangled nerves begin to regroup, and we sit giggling and gurgling and congratulating ourselves on a job well done. The perfect heist, we all agree. A five-star lark. Even Simone is softening up.

From behind a thicket of juniper bushes we all exchange our disguises for more familiar garb. By then Maggie has located a box of sesame crackers and a huge jar of red Romanoff caviar under the rear seat of the wagon. Also a second flask of vodka. My kind of woman.

"Another libation or two and a bite to eat, and then I invite you all to go boating." Maggie waves the full flask in the direction of the lake.

I look up at the sky for the first time since Giverny and realize what a glorious day it is. Perfect for canoeing, I agree, but I remind everyone that Simone and I have work to do. I reach for the portfolio in the trunk of the wagon and transfer it to our Le Car.

"The envelope!" The Judge is staring at me. "What happened to the envelope?"

"The envelope? What envelope?" I ask in a manner that Simone's flaring nostrils tell me is imitation Aggie.

"The one I brought this morning. For the police."

Thus begins the joint argument-search for the carefully typed, superbly-worded statement which, according to the Judge, so beautifully explained the heist by feminists of the highest intellectual quality. No one can remember having seen it since we left Maggie's apartment. Could it have fallen in the street? Could the baker have picked it up? Could it be lying in the gutter in front of the Marmottan?

Now, at any rate, it will have to be rewritten. Written on a grimy scrap of paper Maggie manages to resurrect from her glove compartment. Handwritten by four very tipsy ladies in need of black coffee and a substantial meal. By four giddy Guérillères who are wondering at this point what the heist is really about.

Simone throws herself on the grass in utter disgust. I am not sure if she is going to cry or simply sink into her sewer of vulgarity. I don't have to wonder long. The obscenities are delivered to me in silence by eyes that flicker with fire and brimstone. This she follows by regressing to childish behavior and gorging herself on crackers and caviar. I decide to join her, adding a few good adult belts of vodka.

"This will have to do," the Judge finally says, and hands me the wrinkled scrap of paper.

Together, Simone and I read the message, written in French, of course, in a scrawl, in a hurry, on the hood of the old station wagon:

"We, The Guérillères, hereby make you aware that the security system at the Marmottan Museum, like so many other of your patriarchal enterprises, is a disgrace. Know that we will no longer allow you to misrun any of our cultural heritage. We are returning the art treasure we took this morning to show that our protest is not one of hatred but of hope. Not a product of vandalism but of victimization. You will hear more of us. And more. Until our revolution brings about equality and an end to oppression."

"I don't believe it," says Simone.

"Believe it," I say, ushering her into Le Car in the Mike Tyson manner I reserve for ringside occasions such as this.

CHAPTER TWENTY

"She proceeded to have a tart attack."

Simone continues her hundred-proof-vodka pout as we drive out of the Bois de Boulogne, and we regain the Boulevard Périphérique in silence. I take the Porte d'Orléans exit some twenty minutes later and point Le Car towards the Boulevard Saint Michel. We are soon parked on the rue Guynemer, alongside the Luxembourg Gardens. Not a word has passed between us.

"Coming?" I ask pleasantly.

"No."

"No?"

"No."

God knows how I hate this kind of Aggiesque dialog. I give her a metallic, "Why not?"

"Why should I walk into a trap?"

"What are you talking about?"

"You know damned well."

"I know what?"

"How dumb could I be! Demented. That's the word. Demented. It's all getting very clear. Who could possibly be caught and prosecuted for all this? The Guérillères? Certainly not. They're too idiotic. You? Of course not. You're too slick. But me...."

"Come on, sweetheart. We made it."

"It's my painting, remember? The evidence. So I'll be going directly to jail, huh? Will not pass GO and will definitely not collect my two hundred dollars."

"Or two million, as the case may be."

"You see! You're thinking money. And of running off with mine!"

"Paranoia is dimming your wits, Simone. Your inheritor doesn't collect just because you're in the slammer."

It took her vodka-soaked mind a while to process that.

"You know? You're right!"

"Of course I'm right," I snap. "Aggie's the one who was after your money, remember? You do recall her little lawsuit?"

"It was for something more than money."

More than money? I could really tear into that one, but I opt for peace with, "If I just wanted money, would I be returning this fortune-cookie painting in the trunk? You going to screw this whole thing up, when we're home free?"

"Okay, okay. Look, I know I was wrong about a lot of things. Like the way everybody handled the situation inside the Marmottan. And Maggie is a good driver. Barefoot, that is."

"Damned good."

"But what about the missing envelope? And what about the baker? What's he going to tell the police when the story comes out in the paper? And what about the people in the cars that dodged us when we shot across the Boulevard Suchet? And our tire tracks in the gravel? Do you think the cops aren't going to trace us? Get real, G.B."

"No way. 'Us' have no connection to the baker or the wagon. And the loot is being returned. And the Guérillères, whatever their shortcomings, are no squealers. Even if the *flics* were to catch up with them, they'd be a *cause célèbre*. This is France, remember? Parisians would love them! Any prosecutor would be laughed right out of the courtroom!"

"And *Sunrise?*"

"Take credit for it, Simone. An exquisite copy. A flawless lark."

"You mean it?"

"You did it, Pumpkin." I put my arm around her shoulders and give her a hug. "Listen, this is ridiculous. The two of us sitting here arguing. Come on. Let's finish it off in style!" This I deliver with such flair that Simone produces a wisp of a smile as we get out of Le Car.

I open the trunk and hunch over it. Covertly, I slip Monet's *Sunrise* out of our portfolio, wrap it in the blanket we brought for the occasion, and leave it for safekeeping. Then I grab the handle of the portfolio with one hand and slam the trunk closed with the other. With my free hand I now propel Simone down the sidewalk and through the entrance gate into the Luxembourg Gardens.

We cross the park virtually unnoticed. Most people we pass are either couples or children or their parents, interested in no one but themselves. Just behind the Senate building, not far from the guardhouse, I place the portfolio on the lone bench I had selected long before. Then, while Simone remains behind on another bench just barely within view of the scenario -- to make sure no one walks off with the loot before the guards get my message -- I hurry across the street to a café and phone the police.

Minutes later I rejoin Simone. We sit quietly in the June sunshine, watching the passing clouds, feeling suddenly exhausted.

It isn't long before two guards burst out of the Senate building, walk briskly to the bench and inspect the portfolio. Their lips move with the speed of light as they read the note and exchange comments. How I wish I could hear what they're saying!

Simone shudders as they look around furtively before heading back into the building with the portfolio.

"Did you lock Le Car?" Simone has to ask me then, in her gravelly prophet-of-doom voice.

"Don't do that to me."

"Well?"

We try to look nonchalant as we cut across the gardens and make for the gate and our eyesore-red Le Car. A policeman is standing next to it.

I am suddenly too weak to run. I take Simone's arm and we stagger up to him.

"*Qu'est-ce qui se passe, Monsieur?*" I garble, trying in vain to produce the what's-happening-sir question in my German shepherd voice.

"*Mais vous ne voyez pas?*" Don't you see? he snaps back, with that intimidating growl that the French seem to have encoded in their DNA. "*Il est défendu de garer la voiture ici.*" It's forbidden to park your car here. He points to a small sign down the street that reads no parking on this side of the street, even on Sundays. Then he shakes his head, driving home the depth of my stupidity, and writes me a ticket.

"*Mes excuses,*" I mumble.

We get into Le Car -- which, needless to say, wasn't locked -- and drive off. Nice and slowly, to be sure.

Simone swallows hard, eyes skyward -- her prelude to another Parthian shot. It isn't long before it hits my ears: "You can sure lick ass when you need to, G.B."

"*Merde.*"

"What if it had been a tow-away zone?"

"*Merde.*"

I drive down the rue Bonaparte, past Simone's favorite open-on-Sunday pâtisserie, and she proceeds to have a tart attack.

"Nummies," is all she says. "Want nummies."

Nothing will do but that I should double-park and wait for her while she runs inside.

It is a quarter of an hour later when Simone slides back in beside me, clutching a giant pink package which she instantly unwraps. I count four strawberry tarts, two blueberry, two raspberry and three cherry, one of which she instantly devours. I reach for a strawberry one before I even think to say, "This is insane. Here we sit in the street, double-parked, with one ticket under our belts already, Claude Monet's stolen *Sunrise* in the back, and we sit here inhaling tarts."

Simone licks her cherry fingers. "Compulsive behavior, as the dogs would say."

Well, at least it puts her in a better mood. I drive off, a second tart in my left hand, shifting and steering with my right. Five minutes later we pull up in front of our apartment. Simone gets out, cradling the now messy pastry package and licking blueberry goo from her fingers.

I carefully lift our blanket-wrapped Monet out of the trunk and hand it to her. "I should be back within the hour."

It doesn't take me long to return the rental car over by Les Invalides -- not rented in either of our names but with the phony I.D. we paid big bucks for in the Flea Market -- and hop a taxi home.

Just as we planned in April, we hang *Sunrise* on the ceiling over the bed -- the biggest bed in all Paris, and much fun to jump up and down on while working off excess tart sugar in the bloodstream. This, to the accompaniment of *The Stripper*, which Simone has put on the stereo with the volume turned up to blast. Bouncing and bobbing, we fling our clothes into the air, piece by piece, to fall where they may. Finally, Simone gives a last gleeful jump and collapses, flat on top of sprawled me, lying in wait for her.

"We did it!" I whisper into the coral earlobe brushing my lips. "The perfect crime!"

"Love me?" giggles Simone.

I sink my teeth into her shoulder. It nets me a squeal and then a tooth and nail embrace that leaves me gasping for breath.

Then a knock on the front door stops our breath altogether. The knock becomes a pounding. At the same time a male voice seems to be shouting, in French of course, something like: "Open up! I know you're in there!"

"The police!" rasps Simone. And begins to moan.

I gather all my strength, pry myself out of bed, shuffle into a robe, wobble to the front door, pull it open.

A man, also in a robe, also with tousled hair, shakes his fists at me and shouts what can be loosely translated as, "Turn that fuckin' music down or I'm calling the police!"

I do everything but kiss his feet -- or so Simone tells me a few moments later. She, of course, has been peeking at us from behind the bedroom door. There I rejoin her, and we, in fact, turn the stereo off. Then Simone stretches out on the bed again and tells me, in her empress tone, "Kiss my feet."

And I do.

CHAPTER TWENTY-ONE

"Sht! Zallorfalt! Aluckedup!"

Sunday was yesterday. Today is a far different sort of day. I have been writing all morning while Simone slept. Yes, she was sick most of the night. Nerves, she insisted. Not the vodka. And certainly not the tarts.

Early this afternoon I went out to pay the parking ticket, buy Alka Seltzer, and pick up a few newspapers -- France-Soir, Le Monde, and Le Lendemain. I am scanning them now for news of the heist.

There is nothing in Le Monde. Nothing in France-Soir either. But as I am about to give up with Le Lendemain, an article entitled BOATING ACCIDENT IN THE BOIS DE BOULOGNE slaps me in the eye.

Stiff as an ironing board, I drag myself into the bedroom where Simone is still supine but awake. I translate it for her:

"Paris, July 1, 1985

"It was slightly after one o'clock yesterday afternoon. The Lower Lake in the Bois de Boulogne was sprinkled with families and couples in boats enjoying the welcomed sunshine of the last Sunday in June. Suddenly an uproar came from the middle of the lake, shattering the peaceful spectacle and attracting all eyes to a capsizing canoe. According to Jean-Louis Chefdor, who was present at the scene, four screaming women leaped from the canoe in four different directions.

"Two young men from Tokyo University, who declined to give their names, dove in after the splashing ladies, overturning their own canoe in the melee. But they finally managed to get the quartet safely to shore. There police took the four into custody for drunken and disorderly conduct.

"At the Sixteenth Arrondissement Police Station, where the women were booked, it was disclosed that they were distinguished women of letters. One, in fact, was the well-known Countess Claire Navret, Commander of the Legion of Honor and (so it is rumored) personal friend of a former Président de la République.

"The other three women were distinguished Professor Céline Chantefable, renowned literary critic and author of the recent *Modern Novel: Hoax or Heist?*; Margaret Jefferson Hunt, a wealthy American socialite who has made Paris her home for many years; and Madame Margo Duc, who recently appeared on television in the Philippe Sardou documentary *Great Hunting Safaris.* All four women are to be released today."

I raise my eyes to meet Simone's. She snatches the paper from me, her mouth now an Edvard Munch oval of horror.

"I knew they'd have to fuck it up. Oh, shit, I don't believe it! It's all your fault!" Simone smashes a pillow over her face. "I don' 'eve it! Sht! Zallorfalt! Aluckedup!"

I sit down beside her on the edge of the bed, gently remove the pillow from her face and try to calm her down by saying that not a word of the heist made any of the papers. Using both feet and both hands she gives me a shove that flings me to the floor.

"Look, Simone," I plead on my lower level, "even if the police do put two and two together and come up with those four, they will never rat on us."

"Rat. Aaaaa. Ratso the rat," she moans incoherently.

"Hey, no need for hysterics. They thought we did them a favor, remember? They think we're big on art, big Monet fans, anxious over security, lovers of larks -- "

"Yes, Mrs. Gretch, you've been over all that," screams Simone as she clobbers me on the head with a pillow.

I scuffle across the floor out of reach. "Believe me, sweetheart, it doesn't matter what the Guérillères do from here on in. We're home free. We have the world at our feet." I turn my eyes to the ceiling. "And *Sunrise* overhead."

Simone's eyes trail mine and begin to soften. From across the room I reach my hand out towards her, and she finally points hers in my direction.

"But no more stupid larks, G.B. Promise?"

"No more larks. I promise." I pry myself off the floor and formulate some baby-banter. "Why don't I take you out for some special din-din?"

Simone shrugs. "I'm more in need of tea. And sympathy."

"You got it."

I go into the kitchen and brew a fresh cup of her favorite jasmine tea and serve it to her along with a fortune cookie, whose message I had the good sense to peek at first. In fact, I had to open three cookies before I found something appropriate.

"'You will travel far,'" Simone reads aloud.

That seems to cheer her up. I have half a notion to bring her the Appendix for *The Deposition*, the final pages of which I whipped off this morning while she slept. On second thought, I decide not to push my luck. Tomorrow will be soon enough. Simone's eyes close again, and I collect her teacup and take it back to the kitchen and tidy up. When I return to the bedroom, she is fast asleep. I note that one ear is minus an earring and the other holds a precious Max Ernst silver spur, as I call it. It must weigh a pound and is clearly denting her neck. I tiptoe to her side and delicately remove it. Then look around for its mate, which I find hiding under the bed.

I go over to Simone's Chinese gold and black laquered chest, which I have never opened, and imagine that perhaps the expensive Ernst earrings belong in the bottom drawer which, I vaguely remember, she said has a false bottom, like a safe. I pull it out and see no empty space for the pair of spurs, so I fiddle around and lift out the bottom. There is a shallow space beneath that contains only two objects: a cassette tape and a piece of folded paper. This I unfold and read:

> *"Simone, remember when I bought you this Minton jar? Remembering the good times.... Wonder how long it will be before you will find and read this. Hope you will feel a little of the ole love we had then and wish me a good thought for the day.*
>
> *"It is November 21, 1983, 6:38 p.m. You are in Santa Barbara with Eva. I miss you. Thanksgiving is Thursday and it is a sad evening here, but so good to remember the old times. Now as then, however long it may be before you are reading this, I will always miss you. I still love you.*
>
> > *Aggie"*

I reread it. And read it a third time. Three things are obvious. One: this is precious to Simone. Two: she has kept it hidden from me. Three: she must answer for this.

I go over to the bed and jiggle her pillow. Then again, more roughly. Simone finally yawns and opens her eyes.

"Cheezzeee! What is going on now, G.B.?"

I wave the paper at her. "You tell me."

"What were you doing in my drawer?"

"What was this doing in your drawer?"

Simone props herself up on pillows. "So it's a note from Aggie that I found in my Minton jar when we were packing to come to Europe. Big Deal."

"I could use this in my *Deposition*, you know. It could go in the Appendix."

"Well, stick it up your appendix then," snarls Simone.

I pick up the cassette and wave it under her nose. "And this? More Aggie?"

"Maybe."

"I believe I'm entitled to know what's going on with you and your former lover."

Simone dismisses me with, "None of your business."

"Oh no you don't." I grab her arm as she tries to get out of bed. "I demand to know what this is."

"You feel so threatened by Aggie?" she smirks.

"We're going to hear this," I tell her in my German shepherd voice. "Now!"

"Then let go of me. I need to go to the bathroom."

I step aside, and Simone brushes by. Without as much as a glance at me, she goes into the bathroom and slams the door. I go over to the stereo, turn it on, place the cassette in the slot, and stand, feet spread and arms folded, awaiting her return.

CHAPTER TWENTY-TWO

"If I have to chase you all over this goddamned
planet globe, I'll gitcha!"

Simone has spent nearly half an hour in the bathroom. She now emerges, wearing a lemon-lime négligée. Without a word -- or a look -- she resettles herself in bed in her Madame Recamier pose. I punch PLAY on the tape deck.

We hear Simone's voice say: "Please leave your name and message at the sound of the beep."

Then Aggie's voice: "Hello, Simone. I'm sorry they didn't git to stick me in the jailhouse. You tell Eva she ain't gonna be satisfied 'til they do. I don't know why you had to listen to her. We were gonna be friends. This is stupid, stupid, STUPID! Why Eva insisted that I pulled a strawfork on you...you both know it's a goddamned lie...her trying to shove me off the property like some goddamned bulldyke. And you bein' influenced by somethin' like it, Simone, I don't know what's happened with you. You keep patterning off Eva, you ain't never gonna be remorseful or sad."

I punch STOP on the tape deck and look at Simone. "And this is....?" I ask.

Madame Recamier blinks. "A tape recording of a phone call from Aggie."

"When?"

"How can I remember when?"

"Try, Mrs. Gretch."

"Sometime last year. Probably January."

I arch my eyebrows and again press PLAY.

"Eva? This sheer stupidity of not bein' able to talk! That your big wall of armor? You so goddamned frightened you can't even act like a piece o' humanity? If you was any more shallow, you'd be underneath a snake's belly.

"You know girls, that stupid sheriff told me I musn't harass you, I musn't even try to talk to you, I musn't stop out front of the house. But I can still drive up and down the street, you know. And tellin' him I tried to run you two down out there!

"Too bad those goddamned cops ain't listenin'. They could come here and pick me up and tell me, 'Now, Aggie, you have no legal rights to harass that woman. You musn't talk to her, and she don't wanna talk to you. Legally she don't want to do it, she don't have to do it. Legally you can't do it. Blah, blah, BLAH. That Deputy Ramsfeld's a mean son-of-a bitch, him and all them other fuckin' Palm Springs cops. He even admitted to me that he loved to arrest people."

I punch STOP and turn to Simone. "You didn't turn this over to Mr. Bennett? Or the Palm Springs Police Department?"

Simone shakes her head. "Why?"

"Why? My god, it's evidence of harassment. The police could have put Aggie on probation for it. They would have loved her fuckin' cops remarks."

Simone shrugs and I again punch PLAY.

Aggie rants on: "You listen up, Eva! I've read more and got more out o' books than you've ever gotten out of all yours, and all yer colleges and doctor degrees and what have yah. Gonna git all this said. Then I'll feel better.

"Yeah, Eva. You've tried to git rid o' me, haven't yah? Tried to git me shot through the head with a false goddamned report that I was armed, and you both knew the gun and stuff was in the house. You two holed up there, afraid I'd bust a window and shoot you both? Yeah, that's what you deserve, Eva. Simone, your mother'd turn over in her grave if she knew what you bin doin'.

156

"Eva, you ever lay a finger on Simone, and I promise you I'll gitcha. One time or another. One way or another. If I have to chase you all over this goddamned planet globe, I'll gitcha. And when I gitcha -- or when my friends gitcha, if I should happen to die off or whatever in the chase -- I'll tell you somethin': you'll be left next to dead. Not dead, but next to it, Eva."

With that I punch STOP and glower at Simone. She squirms about a bit and stares up at *Sunrise*.

"Nothing to say?" I growl.

"What's there to say?"

"That woman's out to kill me? And you have nothing to say?"

"She's just barking off at the mouth. Go ahead. Listen to the rest of it. See for yourself."

I punch PLAY.

"You know, you put me through a livin' nightmare, Simone. A livin' hell. And when you did do me the courtesy of talkin' to me, you had only one thing to say: go, go, GO! Get out o' my life! GET OUT O' MY LIFE! For what reason, Simone? I had no intention of keepin' you two girls apart. How can you be so small that you can't carry on two relationships at a time? Eva won't let you? You two itty bitty girls. Two great big grown girls actin' like itty bitty babies.

"Eva? You keep it up and you better be scared o' me, 'cause you make me mad! And I can be bad if I wanna be. You know, girls, worms turn. First they go one way for awhile and then they turn around and come back. And you're gonna be the losers. Not Aggie. Girls, the trouble with all you kind o' people, you jist gotta hurt everybody. Simone, I coulda had that new art studio all done fer you by now. Garage sale coulda gone over. And instead you had to put me through this goddamned fuckin' nightmare. Lost so much weight I'm lookin' like Mahatma Gandhi!" With that I punch STOP and burst out laughing.

Simone makes eye contact for the first time since she

came out of the bathroom. "Still think Aggie's armed and dangerous?"

I shrug and give PLAY another punch.

It sounds like Aggie is taking a long drag on a cigarette before she says, "Eva, I thought you really had a brain. I really thought you were somebody. I was even happy -- and Simone knows it -- that you two got together. I was even gonna move out Thanksgiving and let you have the house for the week-end. And I lost Simone 'cause o' you, Eva, you and your stupid bulldyke mind. Your mother probably figures she kept the afterbirth and threw the kid away.

"You know, girls, there's a lil' ol' God up there in heaven. He looks on all these things for awhile, lets people git a good runnin' start and gives 'em plenty o' rope, and then they hang themselves. And Eva, that goddamned lariat that's around yer neck -- that you put there -- is jist gonna tighten up in the sun one o' these days. And yer gonna be chokin' to death. All by yerself. There won't be no Simone there to help yah 'cause she's gonna git to hatin' you. No friends. Not them fuckin' sheriffs in Palm Springs either. Simone, one day you're going to think back and wonder how you could ever have thought you were in love with somethin' like it."

There is a long pause, then when Aggie continues her voice appears to be cracking: "All you girls think about is yerselves. Do what I want, when I want, how I want. And when you don't want somebody no more jist throw 'em out the goddamned door like they was dirt. Garbage. No matter how much they've cared fer you, no matter what they've ever done fer you. No matter what! Jist git rid of 'em.

"Simone, I feel like our fifteen-year relationship was a pile o' shit. I don't know what hit me, with this grand finale you've pulled now. But you be happy. 'Cause now you have someone who can appreciate how, where and when you spend yer money. 'Cause it's gonna end one day soon, and you're gonna hate her worse than you ever thought o' hatin' me. Because o' all the stuff she's makin' you do. Remember, I told you Eva was subtle. And she'll have you doin' things before -- goddamn it -- you know you've done 'em!

"You know, Simone, that goddamned Eva is capable of killin' you! You could disappear over in Europe somewhere and never come back. Fall off a boat maybe. Yah, it'll look jist like an accident. Or she could poison you. Better watch what you eat, 'cause Eva'll walk away with all yer money.

"But Simone, you can outwit Eva any day o' the week if you want to. And that day will come, Eva, when Simone wants to. And you're gonna be a sorry little bastard when this thing is over.

"Eva? If Simone winds up dead somewhere, you're gonna be number one next. You can bet on it. Bet all o' Simone's money on it. And from yer grave, Simone, you'll know what I do to her. You'll never imagine it 'til you see it. I'm gonna ruffle yer hair, Eva, right straight down to yer toenails. Right down straight to yer toenails.

"You listen to me, Simone. That crazy wino's gonna talk you into somethin' so stupid that if you don't watch out, you'll be goin' to the pokey over it with her. You hear me? You're gonna both wind up in the slammer."

After that, the tape is blank. I punch STOP.

Madame Recamier smiles and pats the bed. I walk slowly over and sit down on the edge.

"I'm gonna ruffle yer hair," she tells me, sounding just like Aggie, running the fingers of both hands through my hair, "right down to yer toenails."

With that, Simone's butterfly fingers fly to all parts of me, north-south-east-west, sending shivers from the top of my cranium all the way down to the soles of my feet. I feel a passion for her that I've never felt before, and I let her know it.

My brain is giving me no information as to who's doing what to whom, but at one point my head is apparently banging against the headboard. At another, I seem to have fallen off the foot of the bed. No matter. Simone is uttering love sounds like I've never heard before. Sounds to die for.

Now I lie exhausted, limp as yesterday's banana peel and suddenly starving, yet unable to keep my eyes open. But Simone is still begging for more.

I can only groan and mumble, "You'll have me lookin' like Mahatma Gandhi."

CHAPTER TWENTY-THREE

"I see you have all my wits about you."

"I'm warning you, G.B." This Simone yells from the bedroom. "I'm not taking any more."

I put aside the old Faulkner novel I'm enjoying on the living room couch and head towards the sound and the fury. "What now?" I ask.

It is the afternoon after the morning after, and Simone is lounging in bed in her smashing raspberry négligée, several pages of the Appendix of my *Deposition* scattered beside her.

"Listen up, G.B.," she says. "This is all very depressing for me, don't you understand? And what reader could possibly be interested in Aggie's phone monologue?"

"You're wrong there." I sit down gingerly on the edge of the bed. "After I thought about it for awhile, I realized that your tape recording was the perfect beginning for my appendices. Words from the horse's mouth. Aggie in person."

"That's not fair."

"In fact, I wonder if old friend Bob would publish the novel with a cassette in a back pocket. Hey! There's an idea. Readers could be treated to The Voice!"

Simone gives me a look that blows me off the bed. "Okay, okay," I say, pacing back and forth now a few feet away from her, just out of reach. "By the way, you haven't told me why you brought that cassette with you to Europe...and hid it in a special spot."

Simone leans back on her pillows, and her négligée

falls open. For some reason the words 'raspberry tart' come to mind, but I am silent, awaiting her excuses for such devious behavior. Finally she sighs, and when she opens her eyes she looks immensely sad. Sad like I have never seen her look.

"Why?" I ask again.

She murmurs, "I don't know."

Maybe I should change the subject. I sit back down on the bed next to her and kiss her gently on the cheek. "I do love you, you know."

"Just tell me this stupid novel is over."

"The Settlement Agreement is it. Did you read it?"

"I can't even get through the Complaint."

"In the novel it should be printed on legal paper, just like the original." I pick up the first page, and with hooded eyes Simone scans it with me:

SUPERIOR COURT OF THE STATE OF CALIFORNIA
COUNTY OF RIVERSIDE

ELLE AGNES GRETCH,
CASE NO. 35890
PLAINTIFF,
COMPLAINT NO. 24483
BY NON-MARITAL PARTNER:
VS.
SIMONE FRANKLIN AND

1. *Breach of Expressed Oral Contract*
2. *Breach of Implied Contract*
3. *Support*
4. *Quantum Meruit*
5. *Intentional Infliction of Emotional Distress*
6. *Damages for Rehabilitation*
7. *Conversion*

Plaintiff alleges:
FIRST CAUSE OF ACTION
(Breach of Expressed Oral Contract)

"That's enough, G.B. First Cause of Action boils down to one sentence: as non-marital partners, Plaintiff asserts that in an oral agreement Defendant promised to support her in style for the rest of her life."

"Provide 'living accommodations, medical expenses, automobiles, and financial compensation.'"

"And in return," says Simone, "Plaintiff would 'render services as a gardener, homemaker, companion, and business manager by providing supervisory and management services for the Defendant.' Like that's what I need: Aggie to supervise me."

I point to the next page. "It says here that 'Plaintiff devoted all aspects of her life to Defendant's interest and well-being to the exclusion of her own.' True or false?"

"Very funny."

"You should never have made Aggie executrix of your will and beneficiary of your entire estate. That's what supported her case."

Simone gives me an ambiguous look, half silly, half serious. "Maybe I should never have made you executrix and beneficiary," she tells me.

"Maybe I should take a lesson from Aggie, and while there's still time save myself from being 'removed, ousted and evicted' by Simone Franklin, Defendant, who 'intentionally, willfully, maliciously and unlawfully' changed the lock on the door of the Plaintiff's residence."

"Maybe you should."

"Oh, I almost forgot. The landlady phoned again this morning and agreed on an eleven o'clock appointment tomorrow at the real estate office. I guess the price is right."

"Even if it isn't, I like this place. I want it. And I'm going to have it."

163

I could comment on Simone's I-like-I-want routine, but I simply say, "Good."

"I suppose you want me to put this apartment in joint tenancy?" asks Simone, with another ambiguous look.

"Up to you," I answer with a shrug. "Let's move on to the Second Cause of Action: Breach of Implied Contract."

"You can lump that one with the Third Cause: Support. All more of the same. Aggie wants payment for past services rendered."

"You're forgetting the pick-up truck. She wants the value of the truck with interest at eight percent per annum."

"I suppose I should have given her the truck."

"Why?"

"Why not?"

"Moving right along," I say, flipping to the next page, "we have the Fourth Cause of Action: Quantum Meruit."

"Your favorite, no doubt. Want to translate from the fabulous Latin?"

"Let's cut to the chase: 'As a result of the facts alleged herein,'" I read, "'Plaintiff has been damaged in the amount of $264,000.00 for the reasonable value of her services.'"

"And then we have the Fifth Cause. The Biggie."

"Intentional Infliction of Emotional Distress."

Simone reads aloud: "'By reason of the unlawful ejection from the residence Plaintiff suffered great mental anguish and emotional and physical distress, became excessively nervous, broke out in a nervous rash, and suffered an illness which has resulted in her being unable to eat in a normal manner.'"

"Let's hear it for Mahatma Gandhi," I chuckle.

Simone does not even smile. She reads on: "'Defendant's conduct was without probable cause, and with wanton and reckless disregard for the right, health and feelings of Plaintiff, and with intent to humiliate and oppress Plaintiff, knowing full well that it would be difficult and more expensive and perhaps impossible for Plaintiff to secure a like place of residence of similar quality.'"

"Well, I guess so!" I laugh. "Gardeners and housekeepers don't usually live in million-dollar estates!"

"Aggie would have if she had gotten what she asked for: 'Plaintiff demands exemplary and punitive damages against the Defendant in the sum of $500,000.00.'"

I give Simone a kiss on the cheek. "That would get anybody a nice starter home," I whisper in her ear.

"Including you, G.B.," she whispers back.

"Shall we continue? And hear how the wretched Defendant terminated Plaintiff's gainful occupation? Plaintiff's Sixth Cause of Action: Rehabilitation."

"Let's skip it."

"And the last Cause of Action: Conversion. How the Defendant took property from Plaintiff's possession and converted it to her own use." I nuzzle Simone's nose with my own and giggle. "Isn't that what you always coveted? A bolt of cloth from Jarvis Tinkle, and Aggie's pile of rocks in the back yard?"

Simone brushes my nose away and reads aloud in a hollow voice: "'On numerous occasions Plaintiff attempted to contact or talk with Defendant regarding her personal effects forcibly abandoned at the Defendant's residence, but Defendant has refused and used a restraining order to prevent Plaintiff from reentering the premises to recover her aforementioned effects.'"

I pick up the last page of the Complaint and read: "'Wherefore, Plaintiff prays judgment against Defendants, jointly and severally, as follows.'"

"Yes, I know the rest," says Simone. "That Defendant be ordered to pay sums for the support of Plaintiff as well as damages in the sum of the value of the truck -- "

"Don't forget the interest!" I grin.

"Also damages in the sum of $264,000.00 <u>with interest</u> for services, for lost income, and general damages in the sum of $500,000.00 for intentional infliction of

Katherine E. Kreuter

emotional distress and another $500,000.00 in punitive damages for same."

"And then we have $25,000.00 for conversion of Plaintiff's property. Also punitive damages in the sum of $100,000.00 for said conversion. Plus the costs of the lawsuit and 'for such other and further relief as the court deems just and proper.' Signed Calvin C. Carney, Esquire, and dated February 4, 1984."

"Poor Carney," sighs Simone. "He was no match for P. Crawford Bennett."

"You sound like you're rooting for the underdog." That gets no response from Simone. "Bennett's lean prose in his Answer to Carney's ridiculous Complaint is worthy of the great Flaubert himself."

"More like reading the telephone directory, if you ask me."

"Defendant admits such facts as being the owner of various pieces of real property but denies each and every other ludicrous allegation."

"It takes him three pages. Full of bullshit repetitions."

"'Defendant admits allegations contained in Paragraphs I, II and III of complaint,'" I chant. "'Defendant denies each and every allegation contained in Paragraphs XXI, XXII and XXIII.' It's pure poetry!"

"Oh, right, G.B. So evocative! Such imagery!" Simone blows a puff of air my way. "Such a squirt o' shit, as Aggie would say."

I think it best to ignore that and say, "And so it ends with: 'Wherefore, Defendant prays that Plaintiff take nothing as a result of this cause of action; that Plaintiff pay for all costs of suit; that Plaintiff pay for all other relief this court deems just and proper.' Dated February 10, 1984, and signed by the master himself: P. Crawford Bennett. And in July he already had the Settlement Agreement concluded."

"Do you think it was fair?" Simone asks herself aloud.

"You bet!" I answer for her. "Aggie 'fully and forever

extinguishes her rights and claims against Simone Franklin. From any and all claims, interests, demands, debts, injuries, damages, obligations, liabilities, causes of action, in law or in equity, contract or tort or statutory, as set forth in Complaint No. 24483.' You bet it's fair. Aggie and Calvin Carney are a pair of losers. And you know it."

"But they settled for five hundred dollars."

"You didn't even have to pay that. That was pure charity."

"Pure poetry," murmurs Simone. "Pure charity."

I shuffle the pages of the Appendix together, toss them onto the dresser and say, "The end."

"The end," echoes Simone.

I stretch out on the bed next to her. "I have news, by the way. The Judge phoned earlier. About the boating mishap."

"Oh?"

"She said that the police were suspicious all right, but with the paintings returned and Countess Claire's connections at City Hall, they just got a good scolding. A semiological spanking, as she put it. And you and I are fully and forever in the clear."

"So the heist was hushed?"

"With no public mention of the Guérillères. Too bad for them. But...Maggie has disappeared."

"She has what?"

"The Judge said Maggie was roaring like a lion when they let them out of the pokey at six this morning."

Simone flings a pillow across the room in disgust.

"Wanted a drink, of course."

"And fast! So they all went with her to the nearest bar that was open, and while the others sobered up on *café noir*, Maggie sloshed vodka."

"And I was just getting fond of old Ratso!"

"As for the station wagon --"

Simone gasped. "Don't tell me the police impounded

it with all the disguises in the trunk?"

I shake my head. "Before Maggie stalked off from the bar, muttering something about Henry Miller and their old binges in La Coupole, the Judge stole her car keys. Then hot-footed it back to the Bois, picked up the wagon and drove it back to Maggie's garage. But apparently Maggie still isn't home."

"Great! Now all we need is for her to spill everything during some delirium tremens scenario."

"But who would believe her?"

"That's true. I don't believe her myself."

"Now, for your further amusement, the Judge – being short on sins today -- next headed for her favorite Members Only Club for lunch. There she picked up a pair of twins -- Italians named Paolo and Francesca. From Rimini, yet! Can you believe it?"

"I'm missing something."

"Paolo and Francesca," I remind her, "were the ill-starred lovers from Rimini that Dante met in the second circle of hell."

"Got it. He fainted with pity when he heard their story?"

"Right." I give Simone a wink. "The Judge fed them brandy and chocolate-covered cherries."

"Bet that wasn't all they got for dessert."

I nod agreement. "Meanwhile, the dogs ran off south on vacation."

"To lick their wounds?"

"Such is the news your Cyrano brings you today." I am stretched out full length on the bed now, fingers laced under my head, looking up at Monet's *Sunrise* as I say, "Ummm. Feel that breeze?"

"Ummm. Balmy."

"Look how it's billowing the curtains." I refer here to the white lace curtains on the open living room windows. We can see them from the bed when the door is open, as it is now. "And sniff that fresh air. It's like springtime in July." I turn and smile at Simone. "And so are you."

She doesn't smile back but she says, "I'm tired of being a writer's widow."

"Say no more. We both need a vacation."

"Why don't I rent us a car? We'll bum around Europe."

Simone gets a kiss for that brilliant idea. "But I'll need to mail off the rest of *The Deposition* before we leave Paris."

"Screw *The Deposition*!"

"Bob Guethin is anxious to get the final chapter to mail me the final contract."

"The final chapter will mail you the final contract?"

"I see you have all my wits about you this afternoon. Just think -- when I met you, you didn't know a dangling modifier from a past infinitive."

"You have taught me everything I know. End of quote."

"How generous of you."

"There may be more to that quote than you know."

"Enough ambiguity for one day," I say. "Let's move on to something more tangible, shall we?"

"Ummm. It's about time."

I hear that certain urgency in her voice and survey my banquet-to-be. "Flesh tones go so well with white satin sheets."

"And the more flesh -- "

"The weller they go!" I babble, like a total idiot.

"How would you like me? Like this? Or this?"

I eat Simone's poses one after the other, like a big box of Godiva chocolates. "All of the above," I whisper.

"Love me," she says, in a voice like verbal handcuffs.

I obey.

CHAPTER TWENTY-FOUR

"Not in the mood."

We left Heidelberg early this morning, and I am now at the wheel of our rented white Peugeot convertible, whizzing along the A-4 Autoroute towards Paris. The top is down -- Simone insisted on it -- and she is leaning back in her seat, Irish eyes closed, rosy cheeks tilted to the October sun, long chestnut hair flying in the breeze. My god, she is a gorgeous piece of work!

I glance covertly at her from time to time but get no response. I got no response either when I attempted some foreplay over breakfast in bed in our hotel room this morning.

"Not in the mood," was all she said.

She clicked on the TV instead and watched the news on CNN, something she has become addicted to during these last couple of months driving about Europe. I find this new mania of hers not only puzzling but rather scary. Simone into international news? The Simone I know has only been into Simone, period.

When I mentioned just that to her this morning, she lashed back at me with, "What do you mean, not interested in world news? You just haven't written that into my part."

"Your part?" asked astonished me.

"Part. Role. Script."

"*The Deposition* is finished, remember?"

"But in your head I'm still your character. Someone you think you invented."

I was bug-eyed. "Invented?"

"But I'm not in your invention, G.B."

"Of course not."

"Of course not," Simone repeated, mimicking my calm alto voice. With that, she gave the breakfast tray a shove and bounced out of bed. "G.B., you don't even know you're doing it."

"Doing what?" I asked, my eyes tethered to her svelte figure covered to mid-thigh with my own burgundy silk pajama top.

"You blot out anything I say that's out of character. You don't even hear me."

"You can say anything you like."

"Hear me! Do you hear me?"

With that, she yanked off my pajama top and flung it in my direction, with excess energy of course, so that instead of landing on the foot of the bed it wound up draped in and about the breakfast tray, now part coffee, part milk, part butter and jelly and bread crumbs.

"Oh great!" I told her, rolling out of bed in -- needless to say -- the matching pajama bottoms. "Ever the child, aren't you."

Simone spun around, faced me squarely, and with arms akimbo said flatly, "No, G.B., I am not a child. Not your baby. Not anyone's baby. You wrote me a part, and a part of me played it. But I don't exist on your stage anymore. Can't you get it? I exist apart from you."

"Of course you do."

She mimicked me again: "Of course you do."

"I can't even talk to you anymore." Bewildered, I shook my head and lifted my shoulders up and down a few times and then said meekly, "You're my love."

"I'm more than that," she spit back, pulling on a sweater and jeans. "Let's go back to Paris."

"Whatever you say."

Within the hour we were on the road. In silence. And

171

in silence we crossed the border into France. When I finally asked her if she'd like to stop en route in Reims to see the cathedral, she said no. That was my Big Clue. Skip the great Reims Cathedral? That wasn't my Simone talking. In fact, now that I think of it, it has been some time since I've heard my Simone talking.

I'm going to get to the bottom of all this. I put the Peugeot on cruise control and flashback to July, when I thought everything was still going just fine. The apartment went into the French version of escrow, and Bob Guethin sent me the final proofs of *The Deposition*. Then escrow closed and yes, I was surprised that Simone hadn't put our new digs into joint tenancy, but no matter. The will she made in California after Aggie's ignoble exit gave everything to me, and she hasn't changed that. So far as I know, anyway. But come to think of it, her phone conversations with Mr. Bennett regarding this new purchase were done without my presence. Or input. But not to worry. I know Simone. And she would have no reason to 'step out of character,' as she put it this morning. But she is acting like a stranger. This change in her hasn't been sudden, either, come to think of it. Take our sex life, for instance. It was still heady in Holland. In fact, I can get cross-eyed just remembering that first night in Amsterdam, after I had taken her to the Rijksmuseum, where she took rolls of film and bought voluminous prints and looked suspiciously like she was plotting some new caper of her own.

But by the time we got to Italy -- where passion should have run wild -- I couldn't get past cuddling. And even that stopped altogether in Switzerland. In Zermatt, of all places. Romantic Zermatt. I barely got a kiss goodnight.

To tell the truth, this whole trip has been a major disappointment. Oh, we've wined and dined and lodged in great style, needless to say. Slept in fairytale spots like the Gritti Palace in Venice and the Villa d'Este on Lake Como. Sipped champagne in the Casino in Monte Carlo. Tasted truffles *sous les cendres* at the sinfully expensive Château l'Evêque in Périgord. And hauled bottles of Wynand Fockink gin from Rotterdam to Rome -- all because Simone couldn't believe the name on the label. But let's face it: basically, I trailed Simone around. Yes, I chose the itinerary -- she wouldn't have known where to start -- but I have been, in a sense, lost. Lost without another lark. Without a caper. Plotless in the Promised Land. And nothing -- or no one -- to jumpstart me.

Not so Simone. Oh, no. She has been sketching up a storm. The canals in Amsterdam, the marinas in Capri, the Cathar castles in Provence. And all along the way she has openly coveted Rembrandts and Vermeers, Titians and Boticellis. I had to literally drag her out of the Uffizi in Florence, where she was squinting at a Mantegna just as she did at our Monet last April.

"I detect overtones here, Mrs. Gretch," I told her.

"All I want to do is see this, Mr. Bennett."

But I was lost. I remember saying to Simone yesterday evening, as we feasted on saurbraten and downed giant steins of beer in Heidelberg, "I don't know what's wrong with me."

Her comment: "No more escaping into your plots, G.B. Time to face yourself. Like I've told you before, get real. Get a life."

I lost my appetite and didn't finish my dinner. We walked back to the hotel along the Neckar River -- a lovers' lane if ever there was one -- and didn't even speak, let alone touch.

Simone is now opening her eyes and asks, "Are we there yet?"

And I think: she's just like a child. What she needs today is what she has always needed: direction. But I don't tell her that. I give her an amicable, "Almost."

We enter Paris at the Porte de Bercy, and Simone smiles when she sees the Seine. We follow the quays along the river, and her eyes really light up when Notre Dame comes into view. Then, as we approach our apartment, Simone looks directly at me for the first time since we made a pit stop in Chalons and says, "Why don't you drop me off with the luggage and go return the car?"

In the same flat tone she is using I answer, "I can do that."

And this I do, just as I did the day I left Simone with *Sunrise* and drove away in the red Renault. Now it's the white Peugeot. I put the top up while I watch Simone go into our building with the last of our luggage, and I am half-tempted to just drive away and on out of Paris. Back to Heidelberg, maybe. Or head for Spain.

But I don't. I dutifully return the convertible to a garage over by the Eiffel Tower and hop a taxi back to the Quai des Grands Augustins. By the time I get up to the apartment, Simone is sitting at the dining room table, sorting a pile of mail that apparently she has picked up from the concièrge.

"There's yours," she says, gesturing to the smaller of two stacks, and not even looking at me.

I pick up the top item, a postcard, note the view of Cannes, and announce to Simone that Céline and the Countess send their greetings.

"So when do the dogs get back to Paris?" she says, flipping through several pages of something she has pulled out of a thick envelope which, if I'm not mistaken, bears the return address of Baines, Borman, and Bennett, Attorneys-at-Law.

"Next week," I say quietly, opening a letter with Margo Duc's return address. "And the Judge is picking Maggie up at the hospital tomorrow afternoon," I tell Simone. "After three months in a white-walled room, drying out."

"Poor old Ratso," murmurs Simone.

"Margo says your 'poor old Ratso' is going to go live

with a group of Tibetan refugees in Switzerland."

"You're making that one up, G.B."

"I never make anything up."

"I know. Don't tell me. You just edit your life."

"True."

I next open the *pièce de résistance*: a parcel from New York. I draw out a book whose cover looks like a white sheet of legal paper with numbers down the lefthand side. Large black letters in the center say: **THE DEPOSITION**. Scattered about it are snippets of Q & A, as Simone calls the dialog between Aggie and Bennett: 'Deaf as you could be and still hear.' 'I won't try to trick you.' 'I had a habit of eating myself.' 'I could sue you for this.'

"Yessssss!" I shout, waving my novel at Simone. "Look!"

She looks up, her eyes narrow, and in a low, raspy voice says, "I hope you're satisfied now, G.B."

I slump into a chair. "I don't know what's the matter with you, Simone. Why can't you enjoy my success?"

"Success?" she hisses. "This is where your success is taking you."

Simone gets up, goes over to the doorway where she has left my suitcase and duffel bag, grabs them, and marches into my studio. I can hear them hit the floor before she reappears.

"Sleep well," is next in the series of her Parthian shots. With that, she sits back down at the table and slits open the next letter in her stack.

I stare at her for a long time before I say, "We need to talk."

All I get is another flat, "Not in the mood."

Okay. I can be sullen too. I take my book and the rest of my mail, march into my studio, and slam the door behind me. I toss the envelopes on my desk and, hugging my novel, go over to the window. Outside, Paris basks in all her glory in the setting sun.

I don't know why, but after awhile I begin to cry.

What have I done to deserve this treatment? I whisper to myself. What has blown Simone way off course? Way, way off course. Whatever it is, I need to bring it to the surface. Get it up here where it can be understood. Aha! I think. I've got it! Yes! That's it. That's what Simone needs. Yes, of course! A shrink!

CHAPTER TWENTY-FIVE

"Another deposition!"

It is the following Sunday: October 27, 1985. For the past few days and nights I have been camped out in my studio, trying to walk on water and not make any waves. Trying to salvage my relationship with Simone. I am waiting for the right moment to broach the subject of a psychiatrist.

I have taken yummy breakfasts-in-bed into Simone and admired with her the glorious *Sunrise* overhead. But she seems even to be losing interest in our Monet. On her easel now is an oil painting she is doing of one of the sketches she herself made of the infamous red-light canal in Amsterdam: the C Dyke. Behind picture windows and in front of mirrors sit the celebrated whores, some seductive in silly clothes, others fetching in the flesh. Simone is painting them in post-impressionist style, in the evening, with pink lights playing upon the waters of the canal.

She informed me this morning that she is going back to the Marmottan today. I told her that I too had that in mind, and she agreed to make a day of it together.

An hour later we are sitting once again on our favorite bench in the downstairs of the museum. "Just think," I sigh contentedly, "a Simone Franklin original now hangs before us."

Simone imitates my sigh. "You know what they say, G.B."

"What do they say? Tell me."

"Criminals always return to the scene of their crime," smirks Simone. "And that is their undoing!"

177

"If we ever get caught, it'll be through some unimaginable fluke."

"Maybe it's time for some new and different kicks? Remember Amsterdam, G.B.?"

"I hope you're not referring to the Rijksmuseum. Forget it! Terribly tempting, I know. But security's too tight. Even the Louvre is easier than that one. The Petits Cabinets anyway."

Simone's eyebrows arch. "Really?"

"Trust me."

Her eyes tell me that she has a response to my 'trust me,' but she switches gears and comes up with: "Did I ever O.D. on the Van Gogh Museum! No purse check there! Like, you could smuggle in a copy of one of those small paintings under an overcoat."

"Forget it."

"Did you notice the workman with the ladder outside the second floor window? Who says he was legit? You could have this phony truck, see, and a couple of guys in electrician's garb -- "

"I said forget it." I shake my head. "Time to draw the line. It was a perfect heist, a great summer, we have an apartment on the Seine, your painting is now world famous, *The Deposition* is printed and on the market. What more could we want?"

Simone seems not to hear. "What about the Groeninge in Bruges? No purse check there either."

"Security did seem lax."

"I want the Bosch. Can't you see those three panels of *Laatste Oordeel* on our living room wall?"

I chuckle. "I'd swipe that one just for the title."

"I bumped up against it. Jiggled it a bit."

"And you do remember the voice that came over the loud speaker and called us to the center of everyone's attention?"

"Video camera just needs unplugging. You could handle that."

"Probably."

"You know, G.B., when we were in Venice? In St. Mark's Basilica? That gold altarpiece...halos of pearls, rubies, emeralds, sapphires. All smooth and rounded but uneven. You could tell the replacements, the 'cut' ones. They didn't cut stones in the tenth century like we do today."

"You do amaze me."

"Replacements...." Simone hums wickedly.

"An altarpiece yet! Does your greed have no end?"

"No. And yours doesn't either. We're both greedy and we're both fakes, but I admit it."

"So that makes you less of a fake? Less greedy?"

"Maybe."

I shake my head again, wondering if she is putting me on or what. "Why don't you just paint your own vision?"

Simone gives me a phony, "That's more scary than the heist!"

But I decide to take her at her word and say, "I know what you mean. You'd have to spill your guts out, like I did with *The Deposition.*"

"Like you did? Give me a break! Give Aggie a break!"

"I'm not talking about Aggie. She was marginal. I'm talking about me. My journey to the scary legal ledges. That's what's *The Deposition* was all about."

"It was all about thinking that you're above the law...among other things."

"It was about escaping the herd," I argue. "Being more clever. More imaginative. More bold. Going where no one has gone before."

My remarks as well as my Star Trek reference are lost on Simone. "That guard is getting closer, G.B.," she whispers.

"He's listening. Think he might recognize our voices?"

I am almost sure now that she is putting me on, but I play along. "He's too far away to hear."

"He is not. I can smell his garlic breath." Simone slips one foot out of one pump and wriggles her toes. "Can't we sit down somewhere out of his sight?"

I remember the emergency exit behind the rear wall. "There are some steps back there," I say. "Come on, nobody's paying any attention." We stroll to the rear of the room, slip unnoticed behind the wall, climb a half-dozen stairs, and sit down next to the emergency exit door.

Simone gives me an accusing look. "You know, somebody could have been hiding back here on these stairs when we pulled the heist. Ever think of that?"

"Nonsense."

Simone leans back up against the wall, kicks off her shoes and begins kneading her left instep. "Oooo...that feels good." She begins massaging her toes. "You know, G.B., this would be a perfect place for a guard to observe the whole show, through a hole in the wall."

"Why don't you tell them that up at reception."

"You taught me how to think this way, remember? Like, maybe we should winter in Madrid. Cut a caper in the Prado."

"No repeat crimes, Simone. Tasteless. Unimaginative."

Simone starts kneading her right instep. "But meanwhile you can plot your next forgery."

"Wrong. I'm through with forgeries. Dealing with them is like trading in the commodities market: to win, you've got to know when to get in and when to get out. No, thanks. No more Aggies. I took her down from her cross."

Simone snorts. "Another deposition?"

"She's dead and buried."

"And on the third day she rose again."

"No resurrections for Aggie. But let's hope that my

readers will find her intellectually disturbing."

"Intellectually?" Simone snorts again. "Oh, right!"

"Yes, intellectually. Her logic, obviously, does not interface with her brain circuitry."

"Gobbledegook."

"Her brain simply rejects any and all information that's not ego-syntonic. That's what's so intriguing about her."

"Look who's talking!" laughs Simone. "So now the Great Critic comes prancing out of the closet again? I prefer the Great Forger."

"I don't want to be writing my next book in the slammer." I get to my feet. "Why don't we walk on over to the Bois? We could go canoeing. I'll paddle, and you can trail your toes in the cool lake water."

"Humm."

"What do you say? Yes?" I get to my feet, thinking that a soothing row in the lake might be just the right atmosphere for a calm, cool, and collected discussion about getting her to a good shrink.

Simone is struggling with her pumps. "Is garlic guard still out there?"

I go down the steps and peek around the wall. "Oh, no!" I gulp. "Another heist!"

Simone comes up behind me to see what I see and gasps. In the outer room, garlic guard -- along with several visitors -- is horizontal on the floor, and the two armed men standing over them are now turning their attention to us. Their motions leave nothing to the imagination.

"Come on, Simone. They mean business. Want to get your head blown off?" I take her arm and drag her into the room and onto the floor. "Keep your voice down and lie flat like the others!"

"They're taking my painting!" she groans.

And she's right. I can't believe my eyes. The thieves are removing at least half a dozen paintings from the walls. And among them is Simone's *Sunrise*.

181

I can't resist whispering in her ear, "Another deposition!"

CHAPTER TWENTY-SIX

"Hold-Up at the Marmottan."

"That makes four," I tell Simone the next afternoon. I've just gone out for the newspaper and have it spread before us on the dining table.

"Four what?" she asks, as if I've said something insane.

"Four depositions, of course," I snap. After a poor night's sleep on my couch and a groggy morning, I'm in no mood for her mood. "Have you forgotten yesterday?"

"So what's it say?"

I read aloud the headlines in Le Monde: "'Hold-up at the Marmottan. Nine impressionist paintings valued at over 100 million francs stolen in broad daylight by five gangsters.'" I look over at Simone. "Little do they know that they have a Simone Franklin original. As I've told you, life imitates art."

"And as I've told you, life imitates farce."

"You want to hear this or not?"

"Whatever."

I scan the article and begin to smile in spite of Simone's sour face. "Listen to this: 'It is a little after ten Sunday morning and the museum has just opened. Among approximately forty visitors, mostly foreigners, slip two young men who purchase their entrance tickets like everyone else. They are joined a moment later by three other thieves (one of them masked) who enter one of the rooms of the museum.'" I look over at Simone again. "How do you like that? It's as if I had told them just how to do it."

"Aren't you the clever one."

"Yes, as a matter of fact." I read on aloud: "'Threatening to use their weapons, the five gansters lock the nine museum guards and the forty-some visitors in upstairs rooms. Three of them then head downstairs and depose three paintings, among them Monet's *Impression Sunrise*. Then they go up to the main floor to take down other paintings. The gangsters are perfectly acquainted with the layout of the rooms and choose the paintings without hesitation. Soon afterward a museum spokesperson will say, These are connoisseurs. They knew what they had come for.'" With that, I burst out laughing. "Some connoisseurs! They can't tell a Franklin from a Monet!"

"And neither could you."

"Get this," I go on, ignoring her remark. "'The whole operation lasted less than ten minutes. The heist accomplished, the five men left as quickly as they had come, piling the paintings into the open trunk of a gray car, double parked -- '"

"And with a working radiator and a good set of brakes."

"Well, we got away with it, didn't we?"

"Maybe."

"Remember when I told you about the alarm system not being turned on during the daytime? That's exactly what it says here: it's only hooked up at night 'because there could be false alarms because of the visitors.'"

"That makes no more sense to me today than it did then."

"Oh, no!" I exclaim. "Wait 'til you hear this: 'The inquest is led by the brigade for repression of banditism!' They call it the first time French curators can remember museum artworks being stolen at gunpoint, bank-robber style. Now does that mean our heist was hushed to perfection or what?"

"What."

"If you don't believe it, look!"

Simone looks and shakes her head.

I point to the next paragraph. "'According to the experts, the stolen paintings are considered to be unmarketable.' Except one, maybe?"

"Very funny, G.B."

"'In that light, various hypotheses have been proposed: hiding the paintings for several years in order then to put them on the market, hoping that the affair will have been forgotten, or simply selling them to a very wealthy and maniacal collector who will keep them in his *secret museum* hidden from everyone's view.'"

"Maniacal? Guess who?"

"'Ransoming them to an insurance company would not be feasible, as the paintings were not insured. Some people are not excluding the hypothesis that it was an act organized by a terrorist group wanting to attract the attention of public opinion.' Hear that? They're suspecting some left-wing extremist group."

"You're making that up, G.B."

"Swear to god!" I wave the page in front of Simone's face. "It says here that the Marmottan would have had to shell out $750,000 a year to insure its contents. And they're on a shoestring budget. The guards don't even have walkie-talkies. But here's the bottom line: 'Among the stolen artworks was 'the most famous of all impressionist paintings, the one which, it is said, gave its name to the movement: *Impression Sunrise* by Claude Monet.'" I look up at Simone. "Well, what do you think?"

"I think it sounds like you wrote the article."

"Sweetheart, I wrote the book!"

We both hear the phone ringing. I cross the room to pick it up and hear Margo Duc's doomsday voice. As she talks to me and I respond with 'yes, no, oh no' in my own doomsday tone, I note that Simone's narrowed eyes are glued to me. When I replace the phone in its cradle in silence, I would bet that she would pay me big bucks to know what the doom is all about. So I saunter back to my chair and wait for her to beg. This is what she deserves.

I flip forward through Le Monde and when I stop at page 18 and start reading, Simone starts shaking her head. "I'm listening," she says in her very own doomsday voice.

"Margo suggested reading the obituaries in the papers," I say, scanning the page. "Ah, here it is." I give Simone a capsule version of an article: "Margaret Jefferson Hunt -- " then I interject a few blahblahblahs that she can identify with -- "passed away last Friday in an auto accident in her Renault wagon. It says she was attempting to negotiate Switzerland's twisty Furka Pass on a foggy night."

"Oh no!" Simone looks truly saddened. "Old Ratso?"

"Yes." I go on reading in silence, then tell Simone, "Apparently her nephew, a well-known Washington lawyer, came over to accompany the body back to Boston, where Maggie will be buried in the stately family mausoleum."

"I doubt that Maggie will enjoy that."

"The paper also says that she was en route to a Swiss compound settled by Tibetan refugees in the sixties -- not long after the Dalai Lama fled Tibet -- with the intention, no doubt, of donating a portion of her wealth to their cause." Here I nail Simone with my big blues. "Remember? You didn't believe me when I told you that?"

"So?"

"So I don't lie."

"No. You just have a tendency to warp the truth."

"Warp? How?"

"By seeing things only from your perspective. You don't view events in an impersonal way. You don't see others for who they really are. You remold everyone. Everything."

"That's ridiculous."

"That's why you're always right. Just like now. You're never wrong. How can you be wrong when you see only your own truth? You're like a blind person who's asked to look around them and tell what colors they see. They're incapable.

And among other things, you're incapable of seeing me for me."

"Maybe you just want me to see you the way you see yourself."

"That too." Simone gets to her feet. "You know something, G.B.? I don't think we're going to make it."

I panic. "We can if you want to." I get to my feet also. "It's up to you."

"No it isn't," says Simone, heading into her studio. "It's up to both of us."

I follow. "I'm willing to try. Whatever it takes. How about you?"

"We're a good match in so many ways," she answers, squinting now at the fresh oil painting on her easel. It's her C Dyke series, and I recognize the whore in the picture window. But I don't recognize her leer.

"That wasn't the look on her face that we saw," I comment. "You know? When she propositioned me?"

"Maybe that's not what you saw, but I'm not painting what you saw."

"Truth is truth."

Simone rudely points a paint brush at me. "And I'm painting my truth."

Time to take a different tack. "You know, I've been thinking about us a lot lately," I say, matter of factly. "About how you've been retreating into your shell. And why. And what to do about it." I pause, while Simone dabs some emerald-green paint on the whore's G-string. Then gives her a little same-color eyeshadow. I know that what I have to say could cause a major explosion, but it has to be said. Even if I get a paintbrush in the face or a whole canvas rammed down over my head. I fold my arms and take a spread-legged stance. "What do you say to seeing a good psychiatrist? Someone who could lead you into insights and realizations about yourself?"

Simone spins around, her paintbrush clenched now in

a tight fist. "You're the one who needs a shrink, G.B.!"

"Me?"

"Yes, Mrs. Gretch, you!"

"I've solved my problems. I know who I am. Why would I need a shrink?"

"It's our relationship."

"But you're the one who's changed."

"You bet!" Simone waves her paintbrush at me. "Change is what I want. What I need. I don't want to keep playing my childhood relationships over forever."

"I'm not your mother."

"No. But the pattern is there. I can see now how she tried to control me. By withholding love when I didn't perform the way she wanted me too. Frightening the hell out of me. I've even realized that I developed something of a split personality to deal with her. On the surface it was 'Yessuh, boss.' Down deep it was 'I hate your fuckin' guts.'"

I nod thoughtfully at this revelation. "All the more reason for you to get through this with a psychiatrist."

"Then I could tell a shrink what I'm telling you? That Mommie Dearest used me as her target? To aim all her guilt at me? Shove all the blame on me for her own fucked-up life?"

"Yes," I say, in total agreement. "So you fled into Aggie's arms. Into another abusive relationship."

"That's right, G.B., I did."

"And that's why I wrote *The Deposition* -- so you could work through it."

"No." Simone turns back to her easel and, of all things, dabs a bit more emerald-green eyeshadow on the sitting whore. I am astounded. By this time I had expected paintbrushes to fly or perhaps a palette knife to rip into her painting. "There you go again, warping the truth," she tells me. "You wrote it mainly for your ego. To get published. To be able to tell your arrogant pals that you were a novelist."

"That was only part of it."

"And part was jealousy. Possessiveness." Simone lectures me as she works: "Your need to take complete control over me. Make me see you as my savior. Make me sever all possible ties with Aggie. Feel ashamed that I ever lived with such an idiot."

"Which she is."

"She may be cunning and crafty, but she's not an idiot."

"She took advantage of teenaged you."

"Yes, she did. And we replayed my childhood scenario all over again. Except that she wasn't as mean and vile as Mommie Dearest. Manipulative, yes. But not mean. She's not such a bad person at heart."

I am aghast. "How can you say that?"

"Perhaps by comparison?"

I plop down on the couch, weak in the knees. "What's that supposed to mean?"

"At least she didn't have me classified the way you do."

I shake my head. "I don't get it."

"No, of course you don't." Simone puts down her brush, picks up a different one, adds some mauve color to it and goes to work on the whore's nipples. "It's time you declassified me, G.B. I'm not the person you think I am."

"You don't think so?"

"I know so."

"You think you're replaying your childhood with me too?"

"I know so."

"I know so," I say, mimicking her cool soprano. "I would never abuse you, Simone. Not physically. Not any way."

"That's your problem. You don't even know you do it."

"I have loved you, Simone," I say, my voice cracking with a mix of frustration and anger. "You are the love of my life."

"But that's not all that I am." Simone turns towards me, with a look on her face that I've never seen before. Perhaps the closest to it was when I saw her stare at the two dogs Aggie was herding into the truck that day before Thanksgiving when Simone and I had driven down to Palm Springs from Santa Barbara. There was a curious mix in her eyes then of confusion and compassion. And something like longing. I can't believe what she says to me now, so quietly it's almost a whisper: "Let go the leash, G.B. There's nothing at the other end."

I stare at her, speechless, and only slowly realize that the phone is ringing. Like a zombie I walk back into the living room and pick up. It is Margo again. Céline and the Countess are back in Paris and driving out to her estate for a few days. And why don't we join the party? she wonders. I tell her it sounds like a marvelous idea, and I'll pass it on to Simone, then phone back.

Still the zombie, I wander back into Simone's studio. The whore's nipples are subtle shades of mauve now. Proud. And agressive. And so is Simone.

"*Noli me tangere*," I say, looking from her to her painting.

"There is no other native Latin speaker here," states Simone.

I give her a rough translation: "Let no one touch me."

"You got that right."

Nothing to do but deliver my message: "Margo was on the phone again. We're invited *chez elle*. Céline and Countess Claire will collect us. We can just go over to their place -- "

"You go to the dogs, G.B. I have work to do."

CHAPTER TWENTY-SEVEN

"By Thanksgiving?"

It is the following Sunday afternoon, November 3rd, and Céline and the Countess dropped me off a few minutes ago on the Quai des Grands Augustins. We've had a wonderful five days *chez Margo* and somehow I'm reluctant to go up to the apartment. I'm standing out on the sidewalk, looking up. Wondering if Simone is up there looking down.

I am reminded of my student days again, sitting out on the island in the Seine, in the Square du Vert Galant, looking up at these penthouse windows, longing to live here. And now I don't even know if I do.

I go up to the apartment and get out my key, half expecting it not to work. But no, Simone has not changed the lock, and I push the door open and go in.

"Simone?" I call out. "You home?"

"In here," comes the reply from her studio.

I hesitate for a moment, wondering where to put my suitcase, then march into the bedroom and place it on my side of the bed. The biggest bed in all Paris, which I haven't slept in since October 23rd.

Simone pokes her head in the doorway, catching me in the act of gazing overhead, at *Sunrise*, feeling suddenly immensely sad.

"So how was your week?" she asks, while her body language tells me: A handshake would be absurd. And don't even think about a kiss hello.

"Five star, all the way," I answer. "How was yours?"

"Busy. Good."

"You really should have come along," I babble. "We had a celebration of Maggie's life. Each one telling favorite stories about her. She and Margo go way back, you know. And Margo told of the days when they were young together in Paris, hanging out with Stein and Toklas, and how just before Maggie sailed back to the States one year, she bought a stash of hash from some Moroccan in the Latin Quarter. Maggie lined the false bottom of her steamer trunk with it. She also jotted down Toklas' recipe for brownies. Then back in Boston -- where rumor had it that Maggie had fallen in love with some French count, that's how happy she was always looking -- she got roped into making the alumna-of-the-year D.A.R. presentation to Radcliffe graduates. Guess what she served them along with tea and sympathy? Apparently the president's wife took off on a table-top striptease. Of course, not even the guests told about it the next day. They all thought they had hallucinated the whole show."

"I could have grown really fond of old Ratso," says Simone, heading back to her studio, knowing I will follow. And I do. And not unlike a dog on a leash. That is the unpleasant image that travels with me en route.

There is a new whore on Simone's easel now. I recognize this one, too, sitting in a second floor picture window, peering into a large mirror that juts out from the outside wall of the building much like a side mirror does from a car. And for similar reasons. This one allows the whore to spot prospective customers coming down the street long before they spot her. Selective sex is what I'd call it.

"The C Dyke series?" I say. "Now there's a *double entendre* for you." Then I look more closely at the painting. In the background three shadowy women are playing poker. One is grey-haired, one looks suspiciously like Aggie, and I can hardly believe that Simone has given the third by very own blue eyes.

Before I can comment on the travesty before me, Simone tells me, "We have to talk."

"Yes. Good. I was thinking the same."

Simone cleans the brush she has been working with and says, "Let's go into the other room. There is mail you need to see. And messages you need to hear."

"Fine. I imagine Bob Guethin is trying to force me into doing some book signings, right?"

"Not exactly."

I trail her out into the living room and over to the dining room table, where we pull out chairs across from each other and sit down. Like mature people negotiating at last.

Simone folds her hands on the table. "G.B., this is not going to be easy for you."

"We'll see about that. What's going on?"

"Aggie is going on."

"Has she contacted you? I'll nail her to another cross!"

"Not me. She got in touch with her lawyer, dear Calvin C. Carney. Remember him?"

"Mr. Milk-you-toast."

"Now Mr. Five-hundred-pound Gorilla."

"Say again?"

Simone picks out an envelope from the pile on the table, pulls out a sheet of paper and says, "This is a copy of a letter Aggie wrote him."

She hands it to me and I read:

October 23, 1985
Dear Cal,

Here I am in Tallahassee, Florida, where I been helping my brother Duke in a senior citizen's mobile home park. We been painting trailers, doing some roofs too, plumbing, whatever. Whatever the ol' folks need doing.

But I'm writing this because I'm coming back to California. Taking a Greyhound bus and will arrive in Indio by noon Sunday. Will phone immediately, cuz I really need to talk to you. It's about this book I saw the other day in a house we were painting for a retired teacher. Don't usually read novels, I'd rather read the real thing, but this one struck my eye: The Deposition. Guess you ought to know why. You're not gonna believe your eyes!

Gotta go now. See you in a few days.

Aggie

I look over at Simone. "This is impossible. A ten million to one shot!"

"Looks like you won the lottery."

"Is this your idea of a joke? Not in a million years would Aggie read a book, right? She wouldn't even get within a hundred miles of a review."

Simone shakes her head. "A shrink would tell you you're in denial, G.B."

"She wrote this on October 23rd?"

"And saw Carney on the 27th. And he's been very busy ever since."

"The 27th? The day we were at the Marmottan? The day of the heist?"

"Need I say it again?" Simone shrugs. "Life imitates farce."

This time I don't correct her. "This is preposterous."

"So is this." Simone draws another letter from the envelope which, I now note, is addressed to both Simone and me, and bears the return address of P. Crawford Bennett.

I unfold it and read:

CALVIN C. CARNEY, Esq.
Attorney at Law
31-7196 Avenue 44
Indio, California 92201
(619) 327-1950

October 29, 1985

TO: *Mr. Robert M. Guethin, Senior Editor*
Hutchins & Merrill
493 Spring Street
New York, N.Y. 10012

Dear Bob,

Pursuant to our last two telephone conversations, I suggest you do more than contact the parties implied in the case. Eva Hopfinger (a.k.a. G.B.) is involved in something far more serious than simple plagiarism.

The prosecution will obviously argue that Hopfinger's novel was written with malice aforethought, with the intent of willfully endangering Mrs. Gretch's privacy. Therefore, <u>The Deposition</u> constitutes an imminent threat to her physical and mental well-being. The publishing house -- along with the author -- will be held accountable.

On behalf of my client and myself I wish to thank you for your fine cooperation thus far in dealing with this most   interesting case. The sooner we settle it the better. I look forward to meeting with you ASAP.
Very truly yours,

Calvin C. Carney, Esq.

I slam the letter down on the table. "Carney's out of his mind. Out of his class, too. We'll get P. Crawford Bennett on the stick and smear Cal and ol' Aggie from -- "

Simone is shaking her head at me and pointing to another page from the same Express Mail envelope. "You haven't read Bennett's letter."

I take the page she next hands me and can't believe my eyes:

Law Offices of BENNETT, BAINES & BORMAN
Attorneys at Law
4763 Tahquitz Way
Palm Springs, CA 92263

October 31, 1985

Dear Simone and Eva,

I am enclosing copies of both the letter from Mrs. Gretch to Calvin Carney as well as the one he sent to Robert Guethin -- which Cal no doubt forwarded me in a spirit of gloat. He and I, by the way, have both read The Deposition *and discussed it, and it is obviously a legal loser. Guethin must be well aware of that also, but he no doubt realizes that there are plenty of loopholes big enough for him to jump through. After all, he's innocent. Or so I presume. I would bet on his total cooperation.*

But Eva, I don't see any way out for you. How on earth did you ever think you could get away with this kind of shenanigan? Yours is certainly not a case I wish to get myself involved in. The outcome is too clear. If I were you, I'd just go ahead and plead guilty. And take your medicine.

Best,

P. Crawford Bennett

I look up at Simone. "I'm going to fight this, you know."

"I'm sure you will."

"Maybe I should just disappear in Afghanistan or Mongolia or something. Would you come with me?"

"And we could have the most elegant yurt this side of Ulan Bator? No, G.B. Even before Bennett's envelope arrived, I knew we were history."

"How can you say that?"

"Would you like a cup of tea?" Simone asks, as if I were some insurance person who had dropped by to discuss a deal on a homeowner's policy.

But I keep my cool. "Sure. Why not?"

I am trailing her again, this time into the kitchen. "You know something?" she says, filling the tea kettle and putting it on the stove. "Funny about *The Deposition*.... You kept telling me that working through my relationship with Aggie in that way would heal me. Remember telling me that?"

"Of course. And I was right."

"But your perspective was all wrong. It was you, forcing me to go over it, that brought things to a head. You, oblivious to the pain it caused me. And would cause Aggie. You, doing it to massage your own ego. And here's the bottom line, G.B.: you, manipulating me and my past to take control. Absolute control."

"Nonsense."

"Remember that lecture you gave on French political history? When I was up in Santa Barbara one week-end? I haven't forgotten your quote: 'Power corrupts, and absolute power corrupts absolutely.'"

"So?"

Simone puts cups and tea bags out on the bar. "I want my freedom."

"You have it!"

"The day you leave," she says, reaching for the sugar bowl in the cupboard.

"You've totally lost touch with reality," I tell her. "We're perfect for each other."

"Just listen to yourself talk, G.B. Just for once analyze what you're saying. If you ever do, maybe you'll make some changes. Right now I want out."

"So you're going to dump me out in the street?" I snap my fingers. "Just like that?"

"No. I haven't finished the story. Your friend Bob Guethin phoned yesterday. He sounded like a serial killer, by the way, and like you were next on his list. Didn't you ever tell him anything about Aggie and her lawsuit?"

"You think I'm a total idiot?"

"That wasn't fair, G.B."

"Bob will never rat on me. I have the goods on him,

remember? I wrote the thesis that got him his degree at Yale. And his present job."

"And a nice new lawsuit," says Simone, pouring hot water into our cups. "With no help from Armani."

"He'll wriggle out of it."

"Let's hope so, Mrs. Gretch."

"So when do you want me out of here? By Thanksgiving? Or shall I just go down to Margo's estate week-ends or whatever when you want to be alone? What do you say we draw up a Tentative Agreement? That I get a Peugeot convertible if I have everything out by Christmas Eve?"

"That won't be necessary."

"No, it won't." I pick up the phone on the bar. "I'm calling Bennett right now. I'll talk him into trashing this case and I probably won't even have to go back to the States."

"Forget it. I talked with him this morning. He'd had more calls from Carney and Guethin and was disgusted. No way will he get involved."

"So what am I supposed to do?"

"Go home and get yourself another lawyer." Simone adds a teaspoon of sugar to her tea. "I've written you a check, G.B. For $50,000. It should help with your expenses. Bennett said the more you cooperate, the better your chances will be. But you're accused of a felony. And that's serious business."

"I'll manage."

"I also bought you a ticket back to Palm Springs. Your flight leaves tomorrow."

"How kind of you."

"You can stay in the Palisades house until things are settled."

"That's all?"

"What more did you want?"

"*Sunrise?*"

"You feel it belongs to you?"

"You sound like a shrink."

"Well?"

"You keep it, Simone. Maybe if they ever find your copy, you can make a trade."

"Not a bad idea." Simone lifts her teacup and touches it to mine. "Cheers!"

Katherine E. Kreuter

EPILOGUE

**** Editor's Note:

1) We wish to point out first of all that those readers interested in the details of the October 1985 heist at the Marmottan Museum will find them recorded by news agencies around the world. They may wish to refer, among others, to articles in:

Le Monde: October 29, 1985
Newsweek: November, 11, 1985
Time: November 11, 1985

2) Pursuant to readers' requests, and with the author's permission, the following series of letters has been added to the Y2K edition of *The Deposition*. These represent only a selection of possibilities. Some were eliminated due to repetitious content. And many documents are obviously missing, leaving great gaps in the years 1985-2000. The readers will have to fill those in for themselves.

725 Palisades Drive
Palm Springs, California
December 24, 1985

Dear Simone,

    It's Christmas Eve, but I have no desire to put up the holiday lights here on Palisades Drive like we did last year. Remember? After we got All-of-Aggie out? We had a regular Electric Light Parade going on here -- wound around the palm trees out front, curving around the contours of the patio arches, and we even had candles floating in the pool!

    And then there was that ten-foot tree you picked out at the nursery. It seems like yesterday that I sat here and watched you decorate it. I had made us a roaring fire in the fireplace, and you were dancing up and down your stepladder in that red and gold kaftan that I like so well. If I hadn't fallen in love with you before, I certainly would have then.

    This evening there is no fire, and there are no lights. And there is no one here to talk with. And your phone is mysteriously out of order.

    I want to fly to you -- literally. If only I could hold you in my arms again...if only I could see your lovely chestnut hair spread again on my pillow...I think all would be well again in this world.

    But I am supposed to remain here. Dear Calvin C. Carney, Esquire, has taken my deposition -- that makes for a total of five, doesn't it! -- but it was only what he called 'preliminary work.' Next week my lawyer and I will have to go another round with his foolishness.

    Gina Allegra, by the way, is doing an adequate job, I suppose, as my attorney. In January I'll try not to laugh when she takes Aggie's deposition. (That will make six!!!) Maybe that will lead to another novel? (Ha ha.) But I've told Gina to wrap this absurd case up fast so I can get on with my life. And, I'm hoping, we can get on with ours.

Our phone conversations this past month -- few and far between -- have been very unsatisfying. All I get out of you is monosyllables. Yes, I know, you're busy painting, but really, couldn't you at least give me a little verbal support? Must you kick me while I'm down? You are an accomplice in all this, you know. There never would have been a Deposition *if I'd never met you.*

> *Yours with all my love,*
> *G.B.*

♣ ♣ ♣ ♣

Paris
15 January 1986

Dear G.B.,

I'm sorry you think I'm "kicking you while you're down," but I don't feel that I owe you allegiance at this point. You are ingenious, G.B. You are witty and can be such fun. And I love your derring-do. But there's so much more to you than that. Do you want me to lie to you? I can't do that. I can only tell you the truth: I'm not in love with you anymore. And I don't want to live with you another day.

I've been thinking about returning a phone call from Margo Duc -- who, by the way, was on TV here last week talking about white water rafting in Bhutan. I wonder if your famous Guérillères would be interested in a reverse heist if they knew the truth. What we did was wrong, even if it was one of your dog food in the casserole and nobody knows the difference concoctions. Besides, strange as it may sound, I'd rather have my own Sunrise *overhead. Anyway, her message said that she received the three copies of* The Deposition *that you mailed her -- one for her and one for each of the dogs. Something for them to chew on. (Better than an old sock!) Cave canem! (Like my Latin?)*

Of course I hope things work out for you. And I'm willing to help you financially, but don't expect anything beyond a casual friendship. And that, only if we can respect each other as individuals. I wonder if you can do that, G.B. And I wonder if you will ever realize that it was Aggie's guts you spilled all over your so-called novel, not yours -- as you not too long ago told me. Ergo, isn't she justified in going after you? (More Latin!)

I am remembering what you told your students in one of your classes at UCSB after they had written long, rambling essays. 'Less is more,' you said. Why not take your own advice and keep our contact to the minimum?

Sincerely,
Simone

♣ ♣ ♣ ♣

725 Palisades Drive
Palm Springs, California
April 1, 1986

Dear Simone,

It's April Fool's Day, of all days, and my day to go to court, face to face with that fool of fools you once shared a bed with. Gina tells me the trial could go on for a couple of weeks; I told her that doesn't say much for her expertise. All it does is make her more Big Bucks. Your Bucks! And I do thank you for them, Simone. But I'll tell you something. Money means zip to me. It's your love that means everything.

I just got off the phone with Gina, as a matter of fact, and she's picking me up in ten minutes, so I'll mail this en route to the courthouse.

She has told me to wear a dress, or at least a skirt of some sort, and to be sure to make contact with each jury member with my big blues. What a farce! I did oblige her by buying a three-piece suit -- yes, with skirt -- but I can't promise what kind of REM's I'll give the jury. Gina is afraid they will identify more with Aggie than with me. Well, of course they will! I don't think even one of them has been to college. I'd bet they've never gone beyond Danielle Steele. They're Tabloid People. And they are going to judge me???!!!

This is pure reductio ad absurdum. You think I spilled Aggie's guts out to the multitudes in The Deposition? I changed the names, you know. And who among Aggie's sublime circle of friends would ever even think of reading good literature? They're all marginal illiterates. I'd be surprised if Jarvis Tinkle can write his own name. But this is a Jarvis kind of jury and must be handled with appropriate garments and gestures. (So saith Gina.)

We should have put Aggie in the pokey when we had the chance. And why you refuse to send me that tape recording you keep in your Chinese chest, I don't know. It could have set Aggie up as a liar and a cop-hater, all of which would have been in my favor today.

Well, too bad. Les jeux sont faits. I only wish you were here.

My love always,
G.B.

♣   ♣   ♣   ♣

Paris
5 May 1986

Dear G.B.,

Yes, I am still not taking phone calls. And yes, I received all seven of your letters. I'm sincerely sorry for the way things went for you in court. I could have predicted it, but you never would have believed me.

Remember that drunken night in La Mangerie a year ago when I was spouting off about Patterns Plan? About how you just have to find the pattern, and then everything else falls into place? I really didn't know what I was talking about then, but I do now. The 'Contempt of Court' charges against you -- among others -- fit perfectly into your pattern. What you need, G.B., is a whole new Plan.

Re: the Palisades Drive house. I've already contacted a realtor and will have it up for sale this summer. Don't worry, I'll have all your things put in storage for you and will pay the fees for the next five years. Thank you for making sure (before you checked out) that the pool man and gardener will continue looking after things until I can get back there and make some new arrangements. The sooner the place sells, the better. I lived there with Mommie Dearest, then Aggie, then you. Now it's high time for change.

You say you have a straight cellmate who's a clone of Lorena Bobbitt? And her name is Virginia? That reminds me of what Aggie used to say about her ex-pal of the same name: 'Virgin for short, but not for long!'

Sincerely,
Simone

**** Editor's Note:
The following is a message on cassette, apparently recorded on December 31, 1990, by Eva Hopfinger, a.k.a. G.B., and delivered to Simone Franklin in Paris by Madame Margo Duc.

Well, it's New Year's Eve, Simone. Another Christmas has come and gone, and it's five years and one month now since I last saw you in Paris. In our dream apartment by the Seine. (Rap music heard in background.) Since you won't take calls from me anymore, and my last letters were returned unopened, I'm going to talk to you anyway. At least that way I can get things said. (Muffled voice, as if hand is being held over microphone, says: 'Turn that damn thing down or you're history!')

Like you, the dogs have made themselves scarce during these years, but Margo Duc has been here to visit me. In fact, she seduced one of the guards in this place -- a red-haired, freckled woman about twenty years Margo's junior -- and they spent a kinky week-end in Las Vegas. Margo told me later that it wasn't her kind of fling, though. Too heavy on the handcuffs....

Have you any idea how difficult these times have been for me? I don't know what I would have done had it not been for the paper and pens the aforementioned matron has brought me. Needless to say, I always distill experience into something creative, and this has been some experience! One day maybe you'll read my scribbles and weep. Don't ever, EVER say again that I don't spill my guts all over the pages of my manuscripts.

Not that you're interested, but I have another new roommate. This one adores the most hideous music. One of these days I'm going to smash her stereo on the toilet here if she keeps it up....

As for Virginia, don't even ask!

Such are my trials and tribulations, Simone. But as I say, I shall transform them into art. And when I get back on my feet... Aggie, look out! I'm going to have a few scores to settle.

Would you please have the kindness to at least reply to this message? I can't tell you how much even a postcard that says 'Hi!' would mean to me.

Simone? Please?

♣ ♣ ♣ ♣

Paris
27 January 1991

Dear G.B.,

Yes, I can imagine. The past four-plus years in the slammer have been very difficult for you. And the fact that Aggie put you there is the hardest (gall) stone for you to swallow. But take my advice: forget her. And listen to me when I tell you that it's best for both of us to go our own ways now. How can you expect me to continue this relationship? How long do you think I'm supposed to share your mistakes? Forever?

I don't know whether you've heard about it or not, but all nine of the paintings stolen from the Marmottan when we were there were found last month in Corsica. Some say in a farmhouse, some say in the basement of a bar. The authorities are keeping the details to themselves. But apparently there was a tip-off to the police, ransom money exchanged, location given, no questions asked. (****)

And I trust there will be no questions asked on your part, either, about anything, when I tell you that with Margo's help I, too, have made a similar switch.... (You don't need to get involved in any more depositions....)

You know something else? I've finally realized what your tragic flaw really is -- more than underestimating people or putting yourself above the law. You wanted to be my narrator, G.B. Yes! My narrator! Wanted to be in total control of your character: me. You wrote my story, past and present. And I let you. But the future belongs to me. From now on, I'm my own narrator.

I am leaving Paris, by the way, to relocate in New York. I wish you well and hope you succeed with your writing. But please don't attempt to make any further contact with me. I won't let you. That's my New Year's resolution. Time to get yourself another pen pal.

Farewell,
Simone

**** Editor's note:
Interested readers may contact the Marmottan Museum for further information concerning the return of the stolen paintings mentioned above. They should also note that the security system there was upgraded during the weeks following the October 1985 heist, hopefully making it impossible for future robberies to take place.

Law Offices of
BENNETT, BAINES & BOHRMAN
Attorneys at Law
4763 Tahquitz Way
Palm Springs, California
92263

June 20, 1991

Dear Eva,

Pursuant to her wishes, I am writing this letter to you on behalf of my client, Simone Franklin. I must request that you not continue your attempts to communicate further with her. The expression 'cease and desist' should make our intentions perfectly clear.

It was a pleasure to have met and talked with you during the period of the Ella Agnes Gretch depositions. But as you know, Simone has been my client for many years, and I hope that this note will suffice to protect her interests.

My advice to you is this: Don't push your chances. You underestimated Aggie; don't underestimate Simone. While you have the opportunity now, why not use your time wisely and dedicate yourself to writing a new novel instead of harassing her?

Consider this a final informal warning.

Best,
P. Crawford Bennett

Katherine E. Kreuter

To: Simone Franklin
  c/o Zoyda Galleries
  1441 Third Avenue
  New York, NY 10003

September 10, 1999

Dear Simone,

My neighbor gave me a New Yorker magazine the other day because it had an article in it on fancy floring, and I just happened to notice a Zoyda Galeries ad about your exhibit. The Canals of Amsterdam, it says here. So will hope this gets to you via the gallery. 'Cuz if you're ever out to California again, you could stop in for coffee or something.

I been living in a house in Palm Springs I bought a few years back -- with money I got from my lawsuit with Eva. Did you know she had money stashed away? Wonder where she got it? Anyhoo, my realtor said this place belonged to the Andrews Sisters in Days of Yore. Remember them? You wouldn't believe the parties I been throwing here. I got Jarvis Tinkle living out in the guest house. His old lady passed a few months ago, so he's glad for the company. Helps me out a lot, besides. We keep busy repairing the roof, painting, doing the plumbing, whatever. My brother Duke is gonna be moving here from Florida before the year's out. Be a regular Grand Central Station!

Remember, Simone, you're always welcome, too. You didn't believe me, after that Eva got hold of you, but I loved you. Still do. And I miss you.

Aggie

P.S.

    Saw this a few years back in the Pen Pals Wanted section of Silver Linings, that Lesbian Connections Club magazine, and I had to cut it out and save it. Just for laffs. As usual, there was half a dozen letters from inmates in Chowchilla. My old aunt Lizzie used to work in the kitchen there, did I ever tell you that? She could put out a spagetti (spelling?) dinner for a few hunerd people and think nothing of it! Anyway, here's the Pal Wanted ad I thought you might want to write to. (Haha.) Or maybe I should? (Hahaha.) I wonder if she's still there?

        Tall brunette, creative, well-educated,
        loves fun, art and literature, music, travel,
        looking for like-minded pal. Will be out of
        here soon and we could meet. Tell me about
        your young self.
        G.B #3856740 Chowchilla, CA 97604

THE END

More Fiction to Stir the Imagination
From Rising Tide Press

CLOUD NINE AFFAIR $11.99
Katherine E. Kreuter
Christine Grandy – rebellious, wealthy, twenty-something – has
disappeared, along with her lover Monica Ward. Desperate to bring her
home, Christine's millionaire father hires Paige Taylor. But the trail to
Christine is mined with obstacles, while powerful enemies plot to
eliminate her. Eventually, Paige discovers that this mission is far more
dangerous than she dreamed. A witty, sophisticated mystery by the
best-selling author of *Fool Me Once*, filled with colorful characters, plot
twists, and romance.

STORM RISING $12.00
Linda Kay Silva
The excitement continues in this wonderful continuation of *TROPICAL
STORM*. Join Megan and Connie as they set out to find Delta and bring
her home. The meaning of friendship and love is explored as Delta,
Connie, Megan and friends struggle to stay alive and stop General
Zahn. Again the Costa Rican Rain Forest is the setting for another fast-
paced action adventure. Storm fans won't want to miss this next
installment in the Delta Stevens Mystery Series.

TROPICAL STORM $11.99
Linda Kay Silva
Another winning, action-packed adventure featuring smart and sassy
heroines, an exotic jungle setting, and a plot with more twists and turns
than a coiled cobra. Megan has disappeared into the Costa Rican rain
forest and it's up to Delta and Connie to find her. Can they reach
Megan before it's too late? Will Storm risk everything to save the
woman she loves? Fast-paced, full of wonderful characters and
surprises. Not to be missed.

CALLED TO KILL $12.00
Joan Albarella
Nikki Barnes, Reverend, teacher and Vietnam Vet is once again
entangled in a complex web of murder and drugs when her past collides
with the present. Set in the rainy spring of Buffalo, Dr. Ginni Clayton and
her friend Magpie add spice and romance as Nikki tries to solve the
mystery that puts her own life in danger. A fun and exciting read.

AGENDA FOR MURDER $11.99
Joan Albarella
A compelling mystery about the legacies of love and war, set on a
sleepy college campus. Though haunted by memories of her tour of
duty in Vietnam, Nikki Barnes is finally putting back the pieces of her
life, only to collide with murder and betrayal.

ONE SUMMER NIGHT $12.00
Gerri Hill
Johanna Marshall doesn't usually fall into bed with someone she just
met, but Kelly Sambino isn't just anyone. Hurt by love and labeled a
womanizer, can these two women learn to trust one another and let love
find its way?

WHEN ITS LOVE $12.00
Beverly Shearer   avail 10/00
Melia Ellis thought what she and Dana had was love. But must love
hurt? Must fearing one's partner be a part of a relationship? Enter
Parker McCallem, a woman from another time – literally, who teaches
Melia the meaning of true love. A tender love story weaving together
elements from today's high tech world with the old west.

BY THE SEA SHORE $12.00
Sandra Morris   avail 10/00
A quiet retreat turns into more investigative work for Jess Shore in the
summer town of Provincetown, MA. This page-turner mystery will keep
you entertained as Jess struggles with her individuality while solving an
attempted murder case.

AND LOVE CAME CALLING $11.99
Beverly Shearer
A beautifully told love story as old as time, steeped in the atmosphere of
the Old West. Danger lights the fire of passion between two women
whose lives become entwined when Kendra (Kenny), on the run from
the law, happily stumbles upon the solitary cabin where Sophie has
been hiding from her own past. Together, they learn that love can
overcome all obstacles.

SIDE DISH $11.99
 Kim Taylor
A genuinely funny yet tender novel which follows the escapades of
Muriel, a twenty-something burmed – out waitress with a college
degree, who has turned gay slacker living into an art form. Getting by
on margaritas and old movies, she seems to have resigned herself to
low standards, simple pleasures, and erotic daydreams. But in secret,
Muriel is searching for true love.

FEATHERING YOUR NEST: An Interactive Workbook& Guide to a
Loving Lesbian Relationship
Gwen Leonhard, M.ED./Jennie Mast, MSW $14.99
This fresh, insightful guide and workbook for lesbian couples provides
effective ways to build and nourish your relationships. Includes fun
exercises & creative ways to spark romance, solve conflict, fight fair,
conquer boredom, spice up your sex lives.

SHADOWS AFTER DARK $9.95
Ouida Crozier
While wings of death are spreading over her own world, Kyril is sent to
earth to find the cure. Here, she meets the beautiful but lonely Kathryn,
and they fall deeply in love. But gradually, Kathryn learns that her
exotic new lover has been sent to earth with a purpose – to save her
own dying *vampire* world. A tender, finely written story.

COMING ATTRACTIONS $11.99
Bobbi D. Marolt
Helen Townsend reluctantly admits she's tried of being lonely...and of
being closeted.   Enter Princess Charming in the form of Cory
Chamberlain, a gifted concert pianist. And Helen embraces joy once
again. But can two women find happiness when one yearns to break
out of the closet and breathe free, while the other fears that it will
destroy her career? A delicious blend of humor, heart and passion – a
novel that captures the bliss and blundering of love.

ROUGH JUSTICE $10.99
Claire Youmans
When Glenn Lowry's sunken fishing boat turns up four years after its
disappearance, foul play is suspected. Classy, ambitious Prosecutor
Janet Schilling immediately launches a murder investigation, which
produces several surprising suspects-one of them, her own former lover
Catherine Adams, now living a reclusive life on an island. A real page-
turner!

HOW TO ORDER
Please send me the books I have checked. I enclosed a check or money order, plus $4
for the first book and $1 for each additional book to cover shipping and handling.

NAME (Please Print) _____
          ADDRESS _____
CITY _____ STATE _____ ZIP _____
Arizona residents please add 7% sales tax to total.

Send to: Rising Tide Press 3831 N. Oracle Rd. Tucson, Arizona 85705